THE MOFFATS

OTHER YEARLING BOOKS YOU WILL ENJOY:

THE
MOFFATS

by ELEANOR ESTES

ILLUSTRATED BY LOUIS SLOBODKIN

A Yearling Book

Published by
Dell Publishing
a division of
Bantam Doubleday Dell Publishing Group, Inc.
666 Fifth Avenue
New York, New York 10103

The trademark Yearling® is registered in the U.S. Patent and Trademark
Office.

ISBN: 0-440-40177-1

Reprinted by arrangement with Harcourt Brace Jovanovich, Publishers

Printed in the United States of America

May 1989

10 9 8 7 6 5 4 3 2 1

CW

TO
RICE

CONTENTS

THE MOFFATS

1

THE YELLOW HOUSE ON NEW DOLLAR STREET

THE WAY MAMA COULD PEEL APPLES! A FEW TURNS OF the knife and there the apple was, all skinned! Jane could not take her eyes from her mother's hands. They had a way of doing things, peeling apples, sprinkling salt, counting pennies, that fascinated her. Jane sighed. Her mother's peelings fell off in lovely long curls, while, for the life of her, Jane couldn't do any better than these thick little chunks

3

which she popped into her mouth. Moreover it took her as long to peel one apple as for Mama to do five or six. Would she ever get so she could do as well?

"There," said Mama, "that's finished." She set the blue and white kettle of apples on the stove. She sprinkled sugar and cinnamon on the apples with the same deft fingers. Jane sat with her elbows on the kitchen table and her chin cupped in her hands, watching

her mother and considering vaguely what to do next. Upstairs she could hear Sylvie saying her lines and saying her lines. She was going to be Cinderella in the play at the Town Hall. Joey had gone bicycling up Shingle Hill with Chet Pudge, and Rufus was probably playing marbles down there at the end of New Dollar Street, waiting for him to come home.

There wasn't anyone to play with, so Jane picked up her doll, Hildegarde, stuck her in her knitting bag, and went out the back door.

All the fruit trees in the yard looked inviting to Jane. She had half a mind to climb the old apple tree, sit in one of its forks and do some knitting. But first she would go and see if Rufus or Joey were in sight. She skipped round the house, out the gate, and climbed onto the fat old hitching post in front. She looked up New Dollar Street and down New Dollar Street for a sign of Joey or Rufus. But neither was in sight.

New Dollar Street was shaped like a bow. That is, it was not a straight street put out by a measuring rod. It had a gentle curve in it like one half of a parenthesis, the first half. Exactly halfway down New Dollar Street was the yellow house where the Moffats, of whom Jane was the next to the youngest, lived.

Jane clanked her feet against the hollow hitching post. For the hundredth time she was thinking that the yellow house was the best house to be living in in the whole block because it was the only house from which you could see all the way to both corners. You could see every inch of the way down New Dollar Street to Elm Street where the trolley ran. When Mama went to town for provisions, you could see her when she got off the trolley, arms laden with bundles and surely a bag of peanuts among them, and run to meet her. In the other direction you could see every inch of the way to Wood Street along which the railroad tracks ran like a river. For hours on end the Moffats liked to sit on the fat old hitching post and count the cars in the freight trains as they galumphed along. Eighty-eight was the most so far.

No. From no other house on the street could you see both corners. For instance, right next door to the Moffats' house on one side was Mrs. Squire's house. Mrs. Squire had no children. Did that make her like the Moffats? Not at all, and she watched them suspiciously. She never would let them or anyone else sit on her fence, though it was a heavy wire one with a flat board along the top, excellent for sitting on, whereas the Moffats' fence, a picket one, naturally was not. Once, however, when Jane had seen Mrs. Squire go out she had sat on the forbidden fence and she had observed that if Mrs. Squire had ever wanted to sit there, she would be able to see all the way to Elm Street where the trolleys ran but she wouldn't be able to see the other end of the street where the railroad tracks were. Not possibly.

Next door to the Moffats' house on the other side was an empty lot. This lot was filled with small mounds of charred and broken bricks, all that was left of a splendid red brick house that used to stand there. The Moffats called it the Brick Lot. It must have been a terrific fire when the brick house burned down but that was years ago before Rufus was born even—and now dandelions and daisies grew between the bricks. As for the cellar, even that was filled in a long time ago and nothing was left of it save a brick fireplace where the Moffats sometimes played at being Druids. But Jane figured that even if there were a house standing in the Brick Lot, its occupants would not be able to see both Elm Street and Wood Street. Only Wood Street.

"See, now, how lucky you are to be living in this yellow house?" said Jane to Hildegarde.

Today was a warm day in late summer. The sky was a rich blue and a slight breeze stirred in the lilac bushes at the side of the house. Jane had that feeling of something good about to happen.

"Come," she said suddenly to her doll. "We'll look at things the upside-down way." She jumped off the post,

stooped down, and looked at the yellow house from between
her legs, upside down. It was wonderful to look at things
from between her legs, upside down. Everything had a dif-

ferent look altogether, a much cleaner, brighter look.

Now she looked between her legs at this yellow house where she and Mama, Sylvie, Joey, and Rufus had lived ever since Rufus, who was the littlest—just five and a half in fact—was a tiny baby. Jane could just barely remember the day they had all moved into this house from the white one across the street. She could just barely remember wheeling her doll-carriage across the street to the new house, for she had been only three years old at the time. Now she was nine.

Joey, who was twelve, and Sylvie, who was fifteen, remembered plenty about the old house, of course. Why, they could even remember Papa who died when Rufus was just a tiny baby, just before they moved to this yellow house.

Jane swung around on her head and toes and looked at the houses across the street from this upside-down position. She made the doll Hildegarde do the same. Peter Frost's house looked spruce and neat and the lawn well-tended. Right-side up the house was shabby and needed paint.

That Peter Frost! If he didn't stop tormenting her and the others . . .

A drawling voice at the gate interrupted her thoughts and brought her to her feet.

"Is this where the Moffats live?"

"Yes . . ." said Jane.

"Then this is the house I want."

Jane recognized the newcomer. It was Mr. Baxter, the odd-jobs man in the town of Cranbury. He was a tall, thin-whiskered man who wore square spectacles over his pale blue eyes. He worked here and there cutting hedges and lawns, doing a little carpentering or a little shingling. Jane eyed him curiously as he entered the yard. She didn't think the roof was leaking again. Mending the tin roof was the only thing that Mama ever hired the odd-jobs man for. Why else should she with four able-bodied children of all ages?

Jane's curiosity turned to amazement when she saw Mr. Baxter march across the lawn, right up to the front of the yellow house. He took hammer and nails from his overall pocket and a sign from under his arm. He placed some nails in his mouth, held the sign against the house with his left hand, and started to nail it on with his right.

The sign read:

FOR SALE

Inquire of Dr. Witty
101 Elm St.

Jane was horror-struck. The yellow house for sale! She clutched Hildegarde tightly to her, whispering fiercely, "It's not. It's not." Oh, why didn't Mama come out and set things right? But supposing even Mama couldn't do anything about this! For Sale! The horrible sign! Mean, mean Mr. Baxter with his hammering! What right did he have?

A bicycle bell rang six times and Jane felt relieved as she recognized Joey's signal. She was glad that at least she would have company. Joe whizzed through the gate with Rufus on his handlebars. He put his brake on suddenly and his tires churned up the dirt. He balanced with one foot on the ground and the other on the pedal. He looked in astonishment at the sight of Mr. Baxter nailing a sign on his house. "Hey, what's the matter?" his eyes asked Jane's

Rufus, sensing adventure, leaped off the handlebars, went up to Mr. Baxter, and said right out, "What's the matter, Mister?"

Rufus couldn't read yet and thought all signs on houses meant measles or scarlet fever.

Sylvie's head appeared in the window upstairs.

"What's all that hammering?" she said. "I can't remember my lines with that noise . . . Hey, what's the matter?" she said, catching sight of the odd-jobs man. She didn't wait for an answer but ran down the stairs and our the front door with a bang, calling Mama as she did so.

Goodness, what was the matter? Mama wondered. Was there an airplane in the sky? A fire? Or just the ice-cream sandwich man? Anyway she rushed from the house, snatching off her blue checked apron and hopping up and down in her efforts not to step on Catherine-the-cat who leaped behind her and under her feet and all around her.

The four Moffats and Mama all stood in a circle. They all looked up at the sign. The children wondered what Mama would do.

"Did Dr. Witty tell you to nail that sign on our house?" she asked the odd-jobs man.

Mr. Baxter gave a final blow to the last nail. He took the rest of the nails out of his mouth and put them and the hammer into his back overall pocket. Then he replied, "Yup. He did."

"Why hasn't he told me anything about this?" said Mama. "We have lived here so long. This is quite a shock. I must go and see him right away."

"Times are bad, ma'am," said Mr. Baxter, nodding his head slowly up and down. "I suppose he figgers he's got to sell. Needs the cash—mebbe."

"Yes, times are bad," agreed Mama.

"Well, good-by," said the odd-jobs man.

"Good-by," said Mama. She went indoors and put on her hat with the blue violets that matched her eyes, and her black cotton gloves. Mama was the only housewife on New Dollar Street who put on her hat and gloves even when she was only going down to Elm Street. She said that was because she had been born and brought up in New York City.

"I won't be gone long," she said. "Sylvie, stir the apple sauce once in a while. It's nearly cooked. Behave yourselves."

Rufus shinned up the hitching post to watch her all the way down New Dollar Street to Elm Street where Dr Witty lived. Then a freight train came along and he turned his attention to Wood Street. He counted the cars hoping this time he would know what came after twenty.

Sylvie ran inside to stir the apple sauce and Joey turned his bicycle upside down. He spun the wheels around and around to make sure the tires were perfect. Jane sat down on the green grass in front of the lilac bush to do a few rows of knitting. But she couldn't keep her mind on her work. Her eyes kept straying to that sign. For Sale! She

16

stared at the sign and she stared at the yellow house. She stared so hard she had to blink. The sign made the house strange and unfamiliar. It was like looking a long time at Mama's face and thinking "This is Mama"; looking and looking and thinking, "Who is Mama?" And the longer she'd look at Mama's face the stranger and more unfamiliar it would seem to her until she'd just have to rush to her, bury her face in her apron, and feel "This *is* Mama."

Now the yellow house with its For Sale sign on it was like that. Janey looked and looked at the house and it just wasn't the Moffats' own yellow house any more. She rolled up her knitting, stuck Hildegarde under her arm, and ran into the house. Perhaps here, indoors, away from that sign, the yellow house would be the yellow house again. She stood for a moment in the sitting-room where the little pot-bellied stove that kept them warm in the winter time was now standing cold and empty. There were the familiar pictures on the wall; one picture of a country girl leading home the cows; another of the big velvet-clad lady whose soft gaze followed Janey's eyes no matter what part of the room Janey went into.

Next Jane marched into the spicy-smelling kitchen. She

17

answered Catherine-the-cat's suspicious glare with an im-pertinent grimace. Upstairs she could hear Sylvie saying her lines and saying her lines again. Did the sign really matter?

She ran into the Grape Room and hung her knitting bag around Madame's black satin shoulders. Madame was not a real person. Madame was a bust. She served as a model for Mama when the ladies Mama sewed for could not come to try on. Madame was built in perfect proportions. She was wonderful! She could impersonate anyone. One day she could impersonate Mrs. Shoemaker, who was so big around, and the next, Miss Nippon, who, as Mama said, was so like a stovepipe. With the help of Madame, Mama was easily able to maintain her position as the finest dressmaker in the town of Cranbury.

Jane looked around the room. There was the yellow plush couch near the window, the same couch on which she had had German measles every Good Friday and Easter for three years in succession. There was the wall-paper with its pattern of bunches and bunches of dark purple grapes that she counted every time she was sick.

"Maybe no one will have the money to buy the house," Jane whispered softly to Hildegarde. "You must remember these are hard times."

She sat the doll on the yellow plush couch. She herself knelt for a moment in the old Morris chair by the window which looked out on the Brick Lot. Even now, in broad daylight, tears of suspense popped into her eyes as she thought of the scarey stories she and the other Moffats made up about the Brick Lot. And suddenly all the warmth and familiarity of the yellow house came back to her with a rush.

"Pooh! What's a sign?" she said. She jumped up. Why, the yellow house was still the yellow house even with a sign on it. The sign didn't change it. It meant no more than when she, Janey, dressed up in Mama's dresses and high-heeled shoes. She was still Janey, she was still Janey. And the yellow house was still the yellow house, she thought in a burst of relief. "For Sale" wasn't "Sold." She ran through the front spare bed-room, back into the sitting room, and out the front door. There was Mama coming back up the street. Janey and Rufus ran to meet her.

"What did he say, Mama?" they asked.

"Well," Mama replied, "he said he just has to sell this house. He has to because times are bad and he needs some money. My, I wish we could buy it," sighed Mama. "But we just can't, so that's that. Anyway very few people are buying houses right now. So we will just forget about that old sign until Dr. Witty actually does sell the house to someone."

So Janey and Rufus and all the other Moffats set about forgetting the sign on the yellow house. At first it was hard though, because every time they came in and every time they went out, there it was:

FOR SALE

Inquire of Dr. Witty
101 Elm St.

2

JANE AND THE CHIEF OF POLICE

AT ONE END OF NEW DOLLAR STREET WERE THE RAILROAD
tracks. At the other end where the trolley ran was the house
of Chief Mulligan, Chief of Police. The yellow house
where the Moffats lived was sandwiched between these two
exciting points. The lawn in front of Chief Mulligan's
house was always the best tended on the street and the two

small mulberry trees on each side of the stoop were always well-trimmed. They were two soldiers, chests thrust out sternly, on guard day and night for the Chief of Police.

When Jane went past this house, she was careful not to step off the sidewalk onto the lawn even one little inch. She tried to remember always to walk, never to run, lest the Chief of Police take her for a thief running from the scene of her latest crime. But she never walked *too* slowly lest she be arrested for loitering. If Joe and Rufus were with her she made them do the same. She warned Joe not to ride his bicycle on the sidewalk at that end of the street and not to ring his bell within several feet of the Mulligans' house. The Chief of Police might not like it.

Rufus had made a scooter out of an old roller skate and a soap box. Jane told him not to ride it on Chief Mulligan's sidewalk on warm days when the tar was soft and he might leave tracks. Once when Chief Mulligan's new sidewalk had just been laid, she had been horrified to see Rufus just swirling around and around on his heel, making a deep hole in it. Chief Mulligan's new sidewalk! She had packed it down the best she could. Then she had run home for a little flour to sprinkle on it in order to hide all traces. Yes—and she had tried to show Rufus what a great risk he was running, doing such a thing.

If she saw Chief Mulligan himself come striding up the street, shoulders back, stomach out, stick swinging to the rhythm of his firm steps, she trembled and wondered what she should do. Should she walk past him in silence, stepping politely aside for him? Or should she just nod her head in a casual, friendly way? Or perhaps it would be better still to give him a polite "How-do, Chief Mulligan."

To tell the truth, Jane was rather reluctant to speak to him out and out. For although *she* knew very well who *he* was, it was not at all likely that *he* knew who *she* was and he might arrest her for being bold. If she did not speak at all, however, might he not think she was pretending she did not know him? That she was attempting to slip past him unseen because of a guilty conscience for some past crime?

At last, however, she had decided that the best and safest course to pursue was the casual, friendly little nod of the head. She'd seen Mama do this occasionally to people she did not know very well. But this little nod did not come naturally to Jane and required some practice before

the mirror. Unfortunately one day when she had experimented on Chief Mulligan with the pleasant little nod, Rufus, coming up the street from the other direction, had asked her why for goodness' sakes she was bobbing her head around in that foolish fashion and making faces at the Chief of Police? Happily Chief Mulligan had seemed not to notice her at all.

But one day, a few weeks after the For Sale sign was nailed on the yellow house, something happened that brought this whole business about the policeman to a head. Janey was trying to balance herself on Joey's stilts. She was leaning against the house, eating a handful of sunflower seeds. She spat the shells as far as she could, trying to better her distance with each shell. At the same time she experienced a slight feeling of satisfaction in realizing that on Joey's stilts she was tall enough to blot out the For Sale sign. So far two people had already come to look at the yellow house. But they were very strange people. One had objected to living next door to a Brick Lot! The other had said that the whole place was too run down.

Now, as Janey put the last sunflower seed into her mouth, her attention was attracted by a new and totally unfamiliar figure walking up New Dollar Street. Obviously he was a person of great dignity. The gentleman held his head, which seemed extremely small in comparison with his stomach, tipped very far back. He wore a derby hat and he carried a cane. Never had such a person been seen on New Dollar Street. Unquestionably he was a person of the highest importance. Who knows? A mayor perhaps? A millionaire? He must have a lot of money in his pocket. He must be coming to buy the yellow house.

Jane spat out the last sunflower seed shell viciously. She spread her arms straight out across the For Sale sign. She was sure not one bit of the lettering still showed. But she held her breath as this elegant person came marching along the picket fence.

"How do you do, little girl?" he said. He tipped his derby hat and nodded his head with much courtesy. Janey was too amazed to return his greeting. He must know her and he must be coming to the yellow house. But no. He reached the gate and marched right past it. And Janey noticed that he spoke in the same way to Mrs. Squire who was weeding her garden, and to Chet Pudge who was spinning his top on the Pudges' white sidewalk.

Jane jumped off the stilts and ran after the man. She felt a sudden surge of happiness to know that this stranger had not come to New Dollar Street to buy the yellow house. She thought it very funny the way he nodded to left and

to right. She strutted up the street right behind him. She stuck out her stomach and held up her head. She tried to copy his courteous air of friendly interest in all the houses and people as he glanced blandly from side to side. Janey had sneakers on her feet so she made no noise. The fine gentleman was totally unaware of the abbreviated shadow of himself that followed him up the street. Jane had mastered his step pretty well, she thought. This consisted of a

slight rocking motion from heel to toe. How it would delight the rest of the Moffats when she got home! Imagine
while they were all waiting for supper that evening! In she
would come, Mr. Importance! However, this jolly idea
came to an abrupt end. As they were passing Mrs. Shoemaker's house, Peter Frost came along on his bicycle. He
stopped beside Jane and hissed in her ear:

"You can be arrested for that."

Horrified, Jane stood still on the heel of her left foot and
the toe of her right. She drew in her stomach and removed
the expression of bland interest from her face.

"I'm just on my way to Chief Mulligan's now. I'll see
that he hears about this," said Peter Frost in a stern voice.
"You see, this gentleman happens to be Mr. Pennypepper,
the new Superintendent of Schools!"

With these ominous words Peter Frost sounded his siren
right in her ear. He rode off making a great noise all the
way up the street so that Mr. Pennypepper had to stand
still in his tracks and place two plump forefingers in his
ears to shut out the noise. Then, shaking his head and rattling the coins in his pocket, he continued on his dignified
way. But with no Jane behind him. Heavens no! Jane had

returned home in the greatest misery.

Of what use now were all the precautions she had taken to treat the Chief of Police with the right degree of respect? What use keeping Rufus and Joe quiet at that end of New Dollar Street and filling in the holes in the Mulligans' sidewalk? What would her punishment be, she wondered. Jail, obviously. How dreadful that would be, she thought mournfully as she disappeared in the enormous lilac bush on the side of the house. Here at least she felt she would have temporary security. This was no ordinary lilac bush. It was a most unusual one. You can't step inside most lilac bushes. But you could this one because its many trunks grew in a circle around a patch of hard, bare ground. Once inside the lilac bush you were certainly well hidden from the rest of the world. Sitting on one of the curling roots that thrust its elbow above the earth was splendid for thinking.

Jane thought and thought, but every thought led to jail. It certainly would have been nice to go in the yellow house and tell Mama about it. "I'm going to jail, Mama." And Mama would say, "Whatever for, Janey?" "For mimicking Mr. Pennypepper, Mama." And Mama would stroke her hair and perhaps even see that she didn't have to go to jail.

But Mama was working hard, cutting out a dress for Mrs. Shoemaker. When Mama was cutting out they must not disturb her unless it was something terribly important like Rufus falling out of the cherry tree. This business about Mr. Pennypepper was probably not quite important enough since she was not yet actually in jail. At this moment her gloomy thoughts were interrupted by Joe who thrust his head through the branches and said:

"Oh, here you are. Mama wants you to go to the store and get some sugar. She says hurry. Here's the quarter."

"Why don't you go? How much sugar?"

"I'm goin' bikin' out Mount Carmel way with Chet Pudge. Five pounds."

He put the quarter on a branch, sprang into his bicycle seat, rang his bell six times, and was off.

Well, of course there was nothing to do but go. Jane put the quarter in her pocket. She left the soft shadows of the lilac bush for the brilliant glare of the midday sun. Her heart pounded. She looked up the street and down the street. She saw no sign of Chief Mulligan, Mr. Pennypepper, or Peter Frost. Safe apparently! She breathed more freely and started for Brooney's delicatessen store. This was at the railroad end of New Dollar Street. It was as far from Mr. Mulligan's house as you could possibly go and still

be on New Dollar Street.

Jane became quite carefree. The day was so bright. Impossible to think gloomy thoughts forever. She forgot all about the police, Peter Frost, jail, in fact all unpleasant things. She skipped up the street in the special way she had of flinging one leg across the other. She arrived panting at Mr. Brooney's and sniffed. She recognized the smells of potato salad, baked ham, dill pickles, sauerkraut, cheese, and coffee. It was very pleasant there. Mr. Brooney was just putting the finishing touches on his bowl of fresh potato salad.

"It smells good, Mr. Brooney," said Jane. "Perhaps you would give me the recipe." She said this as politely as she had heard many a grown person do.

"Give you the recipe? Not on your life. My recipes are my secrets. I'll give you a lollipop, yes. But my recipes, no." He cocked his head on one side and looked at her owlishly over his glasses as he handed her the sugar and a lollipop.

"Thank you, Mr. Brooney. I guess we'll just have to buy your potato salad if we want any of it."

"Yes, yes," he beamed.

Jane peeled the paper off her lollipop with keen anticipation. She stepped out of the store as she took the first lick. Butterscotch! But—oh, my goodness—sakes alive—who was that? Not . . . ? Yes, walking right towards her, not two doors away, was Chief Mulligan himself. He was walking very briskly. No doubt he would snatch her up in a second! So far he had not seen her. His attention was temporarily distracted by Mr. Brooney's little yellow dog, Jup, who kept nipping at his heels.

Jane looked around swiftly. In front of Mr. Brooney's delicatessen store was a large, square box. This was where the baker left his bread early in the morning. Quick as a flash Jane lifted the lid, jumped in, and crouched in a dark corner. She let the lid down gently and listened.

Tramp, tramp, tramp!

"Here he comes," thought Jane, heart in throat.

Closer the steps came and closer. Tramp, tramp, tramp! "Did he see me jump into the bread-box?" So near now that particles of sand kicked up by his feet spattered the bread-box. Tramp, tramp, and they stopped.

"Hello, Brooney," said Chief Mulligan.

"Hello, Chief. Rounding up all the criminals?" Mr. Brooney called out cheerfully from the store.

"That's right," boomed Chief Mulligan. "I'm after one of 'em that disappeared down by the railroad tracks."

"Oh-h-h," gasped Jane. "I suppose that's me."

"Well, good luck to you," said Mr. Brooney.

"So long," said the Chief of Police.

Tramp, tramp, tramp! The heavy steps went on up the street. Jane gave a great sigh of relief. Fainter the steps sounded and fainter. At last she heard nothing but a stillness that hurt. Phew! But it was some time before she could get the echo of those feet out of her mind. When she was convinced that he must be several blocks away, probably at least as far as the railroad station, she cautiously raised the lid of the box a crack and surveyed the scene. How good the sunshine felt! She blinked for a second or two.

"Now the coast is clear," she thought and raised the lid higher.

Unfortunately just at this moment Mr. Brooney came out of the store with his broom and started to sweep the sidewalk. Jane lowered the lid and thought. Should she come out or should she stay in? She liked Mr. Brooney.

He was jolly and always gave her a lollipop or a caramel, but the question was how would he like someone hiding in his bread-box? Probably not at all. She stayed in.

Mr. Brooney hummed a little song as he swept. It was one he had learned in the old country. He sang the same lines over and over, stopping only to speak a greeting to all who passed.

Jane began to feel annoyed. Her muscles were cramped. How nice and sunny it was outside! Oh, if she could only get out. Get out and go home. Mama probably needed the sugar. She would say, "Jane, whatever has kept you so long? You dawdle too much."

But swish, swish, went the broom and Mr. Brooney went on humming his little song. He was certainly very thorough. Jane pushed the lid up a crack and watched him balefully. There now, thank goodness! He had nearly finished. If he only didn't feel he had to sweep the street too. Jane was sure she had been shut up in that old bread-box for hours. She was hungry.

"I'll count to fifty and then I'll come out," she said to herself with determination.

She counted. ". . . Forty-eight, forty-nine, fifty," she

breathed, pushing the lid up again a crack. Sure enough, Mr. Brooney had finished. He turned towards the store, whacking his broom on the bread-box as he passed.

A second more and Jane could jump out. But what was this?

"Hello there, Mr. Brooney."

"Why, Mrs. Shoemaker, how's yourself?"

Mrs. Shoemaker! What could be worse! There was no one, no one on New Dollar Street, who could out-talk Mrs.

Shoemaker. And for goodness' sakes! Here she was sitting right down on top of the bread-box.

"Oh," thought Jane. "Now when'll I ever get out of here? I must think of some plan. I wish I was a ventriloquist."

Mrs. Shoemaker swung her short legs and occasionally kicked a heel against the side of the box. Mr. Brooney whacked his broom on the side of the store. Then he leaned against the fence, happy at the thought of passing a dull hour in a bit of gossip.

Jane felt she had been in captivity forever. She had practically forgotten how under the sun she had ever gotten into this box in the first place. Her eyes grew heavy. The voices of Mrs. Shoemaker and Mr. Brooney became more and more indistinct to her.

"I am a princess locked in a gloomy cavern," she thought, trying to console herself. Then she fell asleep and the black horse that was hers to ride in all her dreams came prancing to her rescue, and she was off—off—long golden tresses flying in the wind.

A clean get-away. Of course there was pursuit. Mr. Brooney and Mrs. Shoemaker, mounted on sorry nags, soon

fell so far behind that in discouragement they abandoned the race. The Chief of Police fared better on a stout red steed belching fire and smoke from his nostrils. But—could he take wing across the lake as could her own black mount? He could not! Hurray! Snorting and panting, the red steed must fight the brambles around the edge of the lake. So he must if the Chief of Police wished to continue the chase. Apparently he didn't though. For as Jane looked back she saw that Chief Mulligan had dismounted. He stood on the shore of the lake and shook his night club after her as she faded from sight. And the red steed sent sparks

40

from his nostrils that disappeared like shooting stars into the still night air. Jane laughed triumphantly at having outwitted her pursuers. She dismounted in the middle of a beautiful clearing in the heart of the forest. Here she refreshed herself with a deep drink from a sparkling spring and sank down into the moss to await the White Prince.

"Have you seen Jane Moffat? She's been missing two-three hours."

Jane woke up, blinking her eyes, her heart pounding. That voice booming above her head seemed at once both near and far away! The voice of Chief Mulligan, of course! Black horse and White Prince faded away. She was Jane Moffat in a bread-box. She heard Mr. Brooney say:

"Jane Moffat? Why, let me see now. Yes, she was here this noon after sugar."

"Well, she never came home with the sugar. Her mother's pretty worried. Now just what time was she here?"

"Let me see now," replied Mr. Brooney, trying to collect his thoughts. "Yes, she was here. When was it? When was it? Eleven o'clock? Twelve o'clock? But just a minute,

Chief. Just a minute. Here's the baker and I have a bone to pick with him. He left me only fourteen loaves of bread this morning and he charged me for fifteen. Hey there, what do you mean?" he asked the baker.

The baker insisted Mr. Brooney must have counted incorrectly. The two started to argue. The Chief of Police stood by with an air of disapproval.

"I tell you," said Mr. Brooney, pounding his fist on the bread-box, "I tell you that I took only fourteen loaves of bread from this box this morning."

"And I tell you I put fifteen in," said the baker, pounding *his* fist on the box.

"Fourteen!"

"Fifteen!"

"Might be you overlooked one," put in the Chief of Police in a masterly fashion.

"Nonsense," growled Mr. Brooney. "However could I do that in broad daylight and all? Still, look in yourself if you think . . ."

Chief Mulligan had become very interested in the discussion. He got out his flashlight so they could see into the corners. Mr. Brooney raised the lid with a grand gesture.

The three men peered in. There was Jane! She looked up at them, blinking. The three men gasped in astonishment.

"I'll be blowed," said Mr. Brooney.

"I'm dodder-blasted," said the baker.

The Chief of Police said nothing. With admirable composure he switched off his flashlight, put it in his pocket, and lifted Jane out. She felt for an instant the icy coldness of his badge upon her hot cheek. She tried to make herself a featherweight and held her breath. For a moment no one said anything. Chief Mulligan gave Mr. Brooney a look which seemed to say, "This is the dispatch with which I am accustomed to discharge my commissions."

Mr. Brooney looked at the baker and said sarcastically, 'Is that your loaf of bread?"

The baker sat down on the bread-box and mopped the flour off his eyebrows in great bewilderment.

Then Chief Mulligan started up the street with Jane still in his arms, his night stick bobbing at his side. Jane stole a look at the Chief's face. He was looking at her. Quickly she lowered her eyes and as quickly raised them again, so he would not think her dishonest and shifty-eyed. She noticed that he was smiling.

"What were you doing in that box?" he asked curiously.

"Hidin'."

"Hidin' from whom?"

A long silence and then very faintly, "You."

"Me!" Even Jane could see he was truly amazed. Could it be he had not been told about Mr. Pennypepper?

"Whatever for?" he asked.

"'Cause I . . ." and swiftly Jane told him about Mr. Pennypepper, jail, Mrs. Shoemaker sitting on the box. Suddenly Chief Mulligan broke into laughter. It started with a chuckle but turned into a loud, hearty laugh. Then into great guffaws. His stomach shook. Tears rolled down his cheeks. He had to put Jane down. He had to sit down on the curb and laugh some more.

Jane watched him in fascination.

"Why, he's nice," she thought.

His face grew redder and redder and the tears coursed down his round cheeks. Jane felt in her pocket for her handkerchief. She offered it to him gravely.

"There are tears in your whiskers," she said.

"Oh-oh-oh," gasped the Chief of Police. He mopped his face and blew his nose very loudly. Suddenly he stopped laughing.

"Little girl," he said, "don't you be afraid of a policeman any more or of anything. Remember this. A policeman is for your protection. He's nothing to be scared of."

Gathering himself together, Chief Mulligan stood up. He smoothed down his uniform, took Jane by the hand. In silence and great dignity they marched up the block. At the yellow house he shook hands with her.

"If I can ever be of any service, call on Chief Mulligan of the police force," he said.

Then he clicked his heels together and saluted.

All the Moffats were looking out of the window and saw him. Jane sauntered nonchalantly into the house.

From that day on, Jane and the Chief of Police were fast friends. She always left a May basket at his door and sent him a Valentine she'd made.

However, she still walked on tiptoe when she passed his house in order not to disturb him should he be napping. And she was still very careful not to step on his grass. Yes, and she was just as strict as ever about Rufus and Joe ringing their bicycle bells at that end of New Dollar Street.

3

THE FIRST DAY OF SCHOOL

THIS MORNING WHAT A HUSTLE-BUSTLE IN THE YELLOW
house! And no wonder! It was the first day of school. Not
only was it the first day of school for Sylvie, Jane, and Joey,
it was also the very first day of school for Rufus. Rufus had
never been to school before except for one day last year
when Jane brought him to her class for Visiting Day. That
day had been more like a party than school, with cookies

and oranges, singing games and a spelling bee, instead of lessons. Aside from that day, Rufus had never been to school before. Why should he have been? He was only five and a half. In spite of this, though, he could already print his name RUFUS MOFFAT and count very rapidly up to twenty.

Rufus was so happy he was going to start school, his face was shining. Jane was going to take him this first day. She was going to show him where Room One was and introduce him to the first grade teacher, Miss Andrews. Rufus was radiant as Mama gave him a final going-over, jerking his red tie in place, pulling his stockings up tight, and tying his shoe laces in a double bow.

"There," she said. "Be a good boy. Do as the teacher says and wait for Jane when school is over."

Then she kissed them both good-by and watched them from the window in the Grape Room all the way down the street. She waved her blue checked apron after Jane and Rufus, the smallest and last of her children to be starting off to school.

"My, my, it'll be lonesome here without any baby around the house," she said as she started to wind the bobbin on the sewing-machine.

Rufus and Jane walked hand in hand. They each had a shiny red apple to eat during recess. When they reached Mr. Brooney's delicatessen store at the end of New Dollar Street, a lively sight greeted them. There was Hughie Pudge, kicking his feet against the big bread-box in front of the store, screaming and yelling, "Won't go, won't go!"

His older brother, Chester, was doing his best to quiet him and to pull him away.

"Come on," said Chet. "School's not bad. You know what Mother said. You don't want to grow up to be a dunce, do you? Oh, well, if you do, all right." And with this, Chet shrugged his shoulders and pretended he was going to go off and leave Hughie, hoping his little brother would follow him. But no. Hughie merely howled the louder. So Chet came back and stood beside him helplessly.

"What's the matter?" asked Jane, while Rufus tugged at her arm, impatient to be on his way.

"Aw—Hughie doesn't want to go to school. It's his first day. He did the same thing last year, howled like this, and it ended by his staying home the whole year. Now he's got to go, Mother says, or else he'll grow up a dunce."

Rufus examined Hughie in amazement. Not want to go to school! Imagine! Why, he had looked forward to this day for years, it seemed to him.

Jane tried to take Hughie's hand. "Look," she urged, "Rufus is going to school. You could go with him. You'll be in the same room. Maybe you can sit together. The teacher's nice. Sometimes she has cookies," said Jane.

"Sure," said Rufus, holding out his chubby hand. "Everybody has to go to school. Even God had to go to school."

For a moment Hughie surveyed Rufus with a trace of interest. Hopefully the three others grabbed him by the arm, thinking victory was certain. But Hughie shook them free and started running back towards home. Way down the street they could see Mrs. Pudge shooing with her apron and making gestures with her arms that meant "Go on, go on!" Jane, Chester, and Rufus soon caught up with Hughie. Jane grabbed one arm firmly and Chet the other and they started to drag him ignominiously in the right direction.

"School is nice," pleaded Jane.

"No, no," screamed Hughie.

"Well," said Jane, dropping his arm in disgust, "if he

doesn't want to, he doesn't want to. We might as well leave him, Rufe, or else we'll be late for school."

"What's this, what's this?" a voice boomed behind them. They turned around. Mr. Pennypepper, the new Superintendent of Schools!

"What seems to be the trouble?" asked Mr. Pennypepper, rocking from heel to toe and clinking the keys in his pocket.

"Hughie doesn't want to go to school, sir," answered Chester, red as a beet.

Mr. Pennypepper put on his glasses and examined Hughie critically. Hughie stopped his blubbering and hung his head.

"Nonsense," said Mr. Pennypepper with an air of finality. "We're all going to school."

He took Hughie by one arm and Rufus by the other. Jane took Rufus' other arm and Chester took Hughie's. In this manner, they all proceeded until they reached the boys' school yard.

Here Mr. Pennypepper left them. His last words were, "Now then, Hughie, I see you have changed your mind. That's fine. But," he said, leaning down and whispering in

Rufus' ear, "in case he changes his mind again and runs away from school, I want you to bring him back. Yes, I want you to watch out for him today; your responsibility until twelve o'clock."

With that he tipped his hat to the four children and marched up the front steps of the school.

Jane, Rufus, and Hughie stood together for a while watching boys and girls arriving in ones, twos, and threes. Rufus felt rather confused and was glad Jane was right there. But now someone appeared in one of the school windows and rang a bell vigorously.

"First bell," said Jane, speaking from experience. "Now I'll have to go into the girls' school yard until it's time to go in. But, Rufus, when we go in, I'll show you and Hughie where Room One is."

And so she left.

For a moment Rufus had a rather queer feeling. All alone. None of the other Moffats. Not Mama, Sylvie, not Joey or Jane. Yes, even Rufus felt a slight impulse to run home and play as he used to. Play what? he asked himself. Mud pies? he asked himself sarcastically. Pooh! He was too old for all that business now. He was going to school. Soon he would be going home to lunch with all those throngs he'd always envied. With something to show Mama too, maybe. Moreover, he had to mind Hughie.

He looked at Hughie who was still a bit stunned at the turn of events. The loud voice of authority that had brought him here was evidently holding him as in a spell which the second pealing of the bell did not even break. And he did not think of rebelling when Rufus grasped his hand firmly and led him into that hated school.

Jane met them in the hall as she had promised. In no time at all she introduced them to Miss Andrews, the first grade teacher, and Rufus took such a liking to her he immediately handed her his red apple.

THE FIRST DAY OF SCHOOL

Room One was filled with boys and girls but Rufus didn't recognize any of them except Nelly Cadwalader who lived across the street from the Chief of Police. Rufus was glad Hughie was there, sitting right behind him. He was glad their seats were on the aisle by the window. They could look out on the railroad tracks. He could count the trains in the freighters better from here than he could from the hitching post in front of the yellow house. But of course he wouldn't have much time for watching trains, he chuckled, if he ever wanted to catch up with Joey in school.

First the teacher asked all the boys and girls what their names were. Then she passed books around to all of them. Readers, they were. Rufus opened his. He liked the smell of the shiny printed pages. He liked the pictures, but goodness! would he ever be able to read those words? Now the teacher was writing on the blackboard. Occasionally the white chalk would squeak. She was making the letters of the alphabet. That Rufus knew.

Oh, he was enjoying himself hugely. All the new smells! First his new book, then the chalk dust whenever the teacher made lines on the board. And best of all this desk! All his own! Rufus liked it here. He turned around to see if Hughie wasn't liking it too.

The whisper he was going to say, "Gee, it's great, isn't it?" froze on his lips. Hughie wasn't there. The seat back of Rufus where Hughie should have been was empty.

Rufus looked at the teacher. N O P Q she wrote in firm strokes. And at that moment, Hughie Pudge, who had been standing behind the big chart that had a picture of Little Bo-Peep on it, walked out the door. Miss Andrews didn't see him, for her back was to the door. Many of the children saw him, but they thought nothing of it. Lots of them had the idea you could get up and go outdoors or even go home if you felt like it. Imagine! Of course they soon learned differently, but anyway, today—the first day of school—they saw nothing strange in a boy simply walking out of the classroom.

But Rufus, along with several others who had older brothers and sisters at school, knew more of what was expected of you. And he knew that Hughie shouldn't have left until the teacher said to leave. What would that man with the loud voice say? He had told Rufus to see to it that Hughie came to school. True, Hughie had come to school. But now he'd left. Did that big man mean that he was supposed to see to it that Hughie stayed in school too? He supposed he did—but where had Hughie gone anyway?

At this moment the bell rang for recess. The teacher carefully explained that recess meant they were all to go out and play in the school yard. It did not mean that they should go home. And after a while the bell would ring again. When it did, they were all to come back to Room One. That's what Miss Andrews said.

"Class, stand," she said.

The class stood up. Then they all had to sit down again

because they all hadn't stood up together.

"Class, stand," said Miss Andrews again.

This time they all stood up the way she wanted them to. Rufus stood in the aisle by the window. He looked out, for he heard a train. The train whizzed past.

"Class, march," said the teacher.

But Rufus was so absorbed with something else he saw down by the railroad tracks that he forgot to march and the boy in back stepped on his heels.

The class had to go back to its seats and again the teacher said, "Class, march!"

This time Rufus marched right past the desks, out the door, down the steps, and into the school yard with his classmates. But he didn't stop there. He kept right on marching out the school yard gate and across Wood Street to the railroad tracks, for what he had seen up there from the classroom window was Hughie Pudge climbing into a freight car stopped on a side-track.

It wasn't easy, what Rufus was going to do, because Mama had warned all the Moffats never to go onto the railroad tracks. But that important man had told Rufus he must see to it that Hughie came to school. He hoped Mama would understand. He would be very careful. Besides, the freight car he had seen Hughie climb into wasn't on the regular tracks. It was on the side-track and would be quite safe. Maybe it was an old thing they weren't going to use again, this freight car.

Rufus climbed up. Panting, he looked around. Sure enough! There he was, that Hughie, sitting on a crate in the corner. When he saw Rufus, he stuck out his lower lip and glowered.

"No, I'm not going back," he said.

"Aw, come on," said Rufus impatiently.

"No," said Hughie.

Rufus sat down in another corner and regarded Hughie with a mixture of admiration and contempt.

"What are you goin' to do here?" he finally asked.

"Watch the trains—maybe take one," replied Hughie.

"Are you goin' to watch the trains forever?"

"Well, maybe until it's dark, anyway."

Rufus glared at him. From across the street he could hear the boys and girls shouting and playing in the school yard. Soon the bell would ring and recess would be over. He didn't know what to do. Should he go back without

Hughie? Or should he stay here with him and try to make him change his mind? Of course if he stayed here with Hughie, he might miss something very important in school. Everyone would get ahead of him. They might start reading in the shiny book.

"Don't you like the shiny book?" he asked Hughie.

Hughie merely shrugged his shoulders. In sudden exasperation Rufus jumped up and yanked Hughie off the crate. But Hughie fought back and yelled so loudly everyone in school would have heard him if an engine hadn't come chugging along—

Choo-Choo-Choo. Choo-Choo-Choo. Choo-Choo-Choo. To Rufus it was saying, "Go to school. Go to school. Go to school."

It was an engine and it didn't have any cars attached to it. Just an engine all alone.

It was slowing up. Now it was stopping just a little way in front of the freight car Rufus and Hughie were sitting in. A lot of steam went hissing up into the air and then the engine started backing up with its bell clapping back and forth. Now, CHOO-choo, CHOO-choo; making a great effort, it backed off the main tracks, backed—CHOO-choo,

CHOO-choo, right back to the old car where Rufus and Hughie were. A slight jar sent the two boys spinning on the floor. A few heavy jerks and a harsh grating noise and Rufus realized what was happening.

"Criminenty!" he yelled, using a word he'd heard that morning in the school yard. "We're movin'. Let's jump."

But Hughie shook his head. "Let's go for a ride," he said.

"We'll get lost," screamed Rufus. "We don't know where this train is goin'. Might be goin' to Boston. We'll be lost."

But Hughie was looking over the side of the freight car happily watching the school-house disappear.

"Lost," repeated Rufus to himself. And a prickly feeling ran up his spine at the word "lost." "Rufus Moffat, 27 New Dollar Street," he muttered to himself. This is what Mama always made him repeat to her when he went shopping in the city with her just in case he might get lost. "Age, five-and-a-half years," he continued and counted up to twenty.

That's what he would do and say if there were anyone to say it to.

However, he soon forgot to be afraid. He forgot about school and the shiny new reader and he began to enjoy the ride.

"You must be the engineer and I'll be the conductor, he said to Hughie.

The two boys looked back. They had left the brown

school-house, Wood Street, and Brooney's delicatessen store far behind. They were crossing the marshes that separated Cranbury from New Haven. Now they were crossing the long trestle over Mill River that emptied into the harbor.

The train was only jogging along—but already they were on the outskirts of New Haven. They could see West Rock, East Rock, and the Sleeping Giant. Now they could see the tall buildings. And now they were chugging down the tracks under the viaduct. Up top, on the viaduct, the trolley from Cranbury ran. So far Rufus knew where he was, for he had often seen these railroad tracks from the trolley car. He knew that soon they should be at the New Haven depot.

But would they stop there? Perhaps they would go right through to Boston.

An express train bound for New York suddenly flew past them, whistles screaming. Rufus' heart pounded with ex-

citement. Hughie's eyes shone. The two boys laughed out loud, jumped up and down and waved their hats.

"Next stop New York!" Rufus cried.

"New York to Boston!" Hughie yelled louder.

They were entering the New Haven station now. Would they stop? Or would they have to go to Boston? Riding on trains was fun but Rufus hoped they'd stop. In Boston they'd be lost —Rufus Moffat, 27 New Dollar Street. The engine was slowing up— Puff— It was stopping—a few violent spasms and the train stopped.

"C'mon," said Rufus, "we better get out."

Hughie was beginning to feel hungry and tired too, so he nodded his head in agreement and the two climbed out of the freight train. There was a man in blue overalls carrying a sooty old lantern and examining the wheels.

"Well, well, well," he said. "what's this? Where did you come from?" The man smelled like kerosene. Rufus thought he looked nice.

"Rufus Moffat, 27 New Dollar Street, five and a half years old. Hughie and me have to get back to school."

The man pushed his cap back and scratched his head.

"Lost?" he asked.

"Not exactly," replied Rufus. "Not yet anyhow. But we have to get back to school."

"You say you live on New Dollar Street? Don't know of any New Dollar Street."

"Sure, Number 27. Chief Mulligan lives on one end."

"Never heard of the man."

"Well, if we could only get back to Cranbury, I could find it," said Rufus.

"Oh—Cranbury. Is that where you come from?" the man asked in astonishment.

"Yes, New Dollar Street," Rufus said.

"Well, I don't see how you got here without no one seein' you. But if that's where you come from, that's where you better go back to."

"If only we could go back on a train, we'd be right at school," said Rufus. "Only trouble is *he* doesn't want to go to school."

The man looked at Hughie. He clicked his tongue against his teeth and shook his head.

"I never," he said. "They ain't many locals to Cranbury this time o' day. But come along, I'll find out."

The man left them for a minute and came back with a time-table.

"Ain't no local for three hours," he said. "Only west-bound train is the Bay State Express, comin' in in three minutes."

As if to confirm this statement, a mysterious voice called out, "Bay State Express— On time. Bay State Express— On time. Track 9. 11:45. Track 9."

"Doesn't the Bay State ever stop in Cranbury?" asked Rufus.

"Never," said the man.

"All aboard Bay State Express! ALL ABOARD Bay State. Track 9."

"Never," repeated the man in overalls. "But who knows? C'mon."

With that he grabbed Hughie and Rufus by the arm, tore down the tracks to Track 9, where the engine of the Bay State Express was hissing and steaming, just itching to be off.

"Hey, Dick," called the trackman to the engineer.

"Hey yourself, Bob," answered the engineer, grinning and leaning out of the cab.

"Listen, Dick; here are two kids—lost—come on a freight train from Cranbury—they gotta be returned. How about stopping thirty seconds to let them off?"

"Couldn't be done," answered the engineer. "Bay State never stops in Cranbury—straight through to New York."

Rufus' heart sank. So did Hughie's. However, they both had faith in this man, Bob, of theirs.

Bob said, "Well, the New York, New Haven and Hartford got them here. The way I look at it, they ought to git 'em back."

"M-m-m," said the engineer, "ask the Station Master."

"Wait here," said Bob to Rufus and Hughie.

Then Bob tore down the station and it seemed only a second before he was back.

Inside the station, that voice could be heard,

"Last call for Bay State Express—Track 9. Bay State Express—Track 9."

" 'Board," cried the conductors.

"He says yup," said Bob, boosting Rufus and Hughie into the engine cab.

Then whistles sounded, a huge blast of steam went up into the sky—the train was off. Hughie and Rufus waved their caps after Bob whom they could see for a second waving his cap after them.

Goodness, this train was just speeding along. Of course, Rufus and Hughie couldn't stand too close to the engineer. But they could watch the fireman and they saw enough to

see that running an engine was a marvelous job.

The express whizzed over the tracks the freight train had taken so long to cross a little while before. Rufus and Hughie could hardly tell where they were. And in exactly three minutes after leaving the New Haven station, the express train came to a stop—the fireman lifted the two boys down—the engineer grinned and waved to them, and off the train went with everybody aboard staring out the window to find out why the express, that wasn't supposed to stop until it reached New York, had stopped in this funny little town.

Rufus and Hughie waved after the train until it was just a speck in the distance. Then Rufus thought about school again.

"Come on now," he said, "we better get back to school."

"Do you have to go to school to be an engineer?" asked Hughie.

"Of course you do. That engineer named Dick, well, once't he was in Room One too," replied Rufus, thinking this out laboriously.

"All right then, I'll go to school." Hughie finally gave in.

And the two boys returned to Miss Andrews' room. They took their places just in time to be dismissed to go home to lunch.

"Class, stand," the teacher was saying.

4

A HORSE AND WAGON

WHAT A SUNDAY THAT WAS! MAMA THOUGHT SHE WOULD
never get them off to Sunday School. Usually this was ac-
complished simply enough. Of course they could all dress
themselves and neatly blacken their high shoes. All Mama
had to do was to look them over when they had finished
to see that all was as neat as possible, maybe to jerk Rufus'
red tie in place. Then the four Moffats might go into the
front yard and play quietly, or better still, not play at all
but read over their Sunday School lessons until the church
bells rang.

These Sunday mornings before Sunday School were very
trying to Rufus. Rufus didn't have any lessons to learn in

73

Sunday School because he was in the kindergarten class Oh, occasionally a picture to color or a little verse from the Bible to learn, but usually nothing.

This Sunday Rufus was having a harder time than ever waiting for Sunday School. He was all dressed up and he couldn't do anything. He would have liked to jump over and over the hitching post in front of the house. Mama did not allow this, though, because he might get grass stains on his white stockings. Or he would have liked to sail boats on the puddles left in the gutter from last night's rain. But Mama did not allow this either because he might fall in. This was not allowed and that was not allowed. Every Sunday the same old thing, waiting and waiting in his best sailor suit for the church bells.

He wandered around to the back yard and gathered up some of the hard, green grapes the rain and the wind had knocked off the arbor during the night. These he stuffed into his pocket in case he should see that Peter Frost. Who knows? He might have a chance to fire them at him.

Then he joined the others on the front porch. Jane was trying to learn her "duty towards her neighbor." She had learned her "duty towards God," but somehow her "duty towards her neighbor" just would not stay in her head. Oh, dear, she would never get out of the catechism class until it did. Already she had been longer in that class than any other girl except Letitia Murdock who was stuck with her "duty towards God."

Rufus sat down with his back to the railing. Jane read her "duty towards her neighbor" out loud for the hundredth time. Then she tried to repeat it from memory. No use! Halfway through she stumbled and groped for the right words. Rufus supplied them for her and on she went.

Rufus knew it perfectly and he was only in the kindergarten! He had heard Jane read it so often, it just stayed in his head without his even trying to learn it. Just like when Sylvie was learning her Latin. "Bonus, bona, bonum." Rufus always got it as soon as she did. Or Joe his history. "First-shot-Civil-War-shot-Fort-Sumter-four-o'clock-in-the-morning." Rufus could say it just like that.

Suddenly Rufus became aware of a damp feeling spreading down his legs. He leaped up! Those green grapes! All squashed! Oh! His best suit ruined!

That was the first time he had to have his suit changed and Mama wasn't any too pleased naturally, busy as she was with the pot roast and onions for the Sunday dinner.

When Rufus was all dressed again in his second best sailor suit and it was nearly time to start for Sunday School, he climbed onto the hitching post to wait for Janey and Sylvie to tie on their hats. He wasn't jumping over the hitching post. He was just sitting on it. Sitting there quietly, staring at his reflection in the puddle, wishing he had a magic belt around his waist covered with push buttons and chains. Push one button and out would come an ice-cream sandwich. Push another and a shower of caramels would fall into his hands. Another and a dish of pot roast and onions . . .

Suddenly, right in his ear . . . Whe-e-e . . .

Peter Frost's bike siren! Splash! Off the hitching post went Rufus! Into the mud puddle! That Peter Frost had approached silently and swiftly on his bicycle. As he sped past Rufus he thought: what fun to startle Rufus with a terrific screech on his siren. So, poor Rufus!

That was the second time he had to have his clothes changed.

Of course Mama didn't like this one bit, but Janey and Sylvie assured her it really had not been Rufus' fault this

time and if Mama herself had been sitting on the hitching post, she too would have fallen off.

At this moment the church bells pealed—the low-pitched bells of their church and the high-pitched ones of Peter Frost's church. It was time to start. Mama kissed each one of them and the four

started solemnly up the street. At last they were off—Rufus in one of his everyday sailor suits.

"Keep hold of Rufus' hand, Joey," called Mama after them. "And give my regards to the Reverend Gandy," she said, waving her blue checked apron, and watching them until they had passed the Pudges.

78

At the corner of Elm Street Sylvie suddenly said, "Goodness, there goes Edie Ellenbach. It must be late. I'll have to hurry to get in place in the choir. Joey, don't let Rufus climb the flagpole on the Green. See you after Sunday School. Good-by."

Then she flew down Elm Street with her curls flying, calling "Edie! Edie!"

The other three stood at the corner for a moment, waiting for a slow-moving horse and wagon to pass by.

"Maybe it's the peanut man," said Rufus, thoughtfully fingering his penny meant for the Sunday School plate.

"Or the flying horse wagon," said Jane, shaking her little patent leather pocket-book to hear her two pennies clink together.

"S'neither," said Joe. "S'the Salvation Army man."

The driver drew up at the curb beside them.

"Hi!" he said. "Which road takes me to Orchard Grove?"

Joe thought rapidly. The road to Orchard Grove led past the Green. Right where they were going. A lift! A ride in a horse and wagon!

"If you'll give us a lift, we'll show you," said Joe. "We're

going that way ourselves."

"Hop up," agreed the man.

Joe boosted Jane and Rufus onto the pile of newspapers in the back of the wagon. He jumped up to the seat beside the driver. What a nice man this was! He gave the reins to Joe without his even asking.

"You know the way through town better than I do," he said. "I'm going to take a little nap. Freshen me up for the meeting at Orchard Grove. There's my drum under the seat. Beat that when it's time for me to wake up. It's the only thing aside from an earthquake that will wake me."

Off they went with Joe at the reins! Down Elm Street,

past the Public Library, the hardware shop, the A & P, to the Green, but not on foot—in a horse and wagon. They waved gaily to Mrs. Shoemaker who waved back at them without a trace of surprise. You'd think she saw the Moffats on horses every day of her life.

When they reached the drinking trough on the Green, Joe said, "Who-a, Billy. Here's where we leave you—I suppose."

Joe sat there a moment, the reins slack in his hands. He had certainly driven that horse well for a beginner, he thought. And that corner where Rock Avenue and Main Street came together was no easy one either. What a wonderful feeling to drive a horse! He looked at the man who was still asleep. He must be dead tired. It was a pity he had such a long drive ahead of him. Over three miles he'd have to go. Straight ahead the road led to Orchard Grove. Over there across the Green was Sunday School. The doors were closed. There was no one in sight. The church bells had stopped ringing. Probably Sunday School had already begun. They would be late. One thing he did not like to do was go in late to Sunday School. Why not drive this man to Orchard Grove instead? thought Joe.

Joe glanced back at Jane and Rufus. They were swinging their legs and had made no move to jump down.

"Hey, how about our driving this man to Orchard Grove?" he asked them.

"All right." Unanimous consent from Rufus and Jane.

"Salvation Army's just like Sunday School," said Jane.

"But Mama might worry if we're late getting back," said Joe. "Let's see now . . . I know what . . . we could leave a message for Sylvie."

"On the drinking trough!" said Jane.

"Yes, Sylvie always stops for a drink on her way home," agreed Joey.

Joe had a piece of white chalk in his pocket among all his other valuables, as almost any boy would. Not a boy like Rufus, of course. Not one who had to have his clothes changed every other minute so you could never count on his pocket collection. But Joe had a nice piece of white chalk in his pocket and he handed it to Jane.

"Write big so she won't miss it," he said.

On the dry part of the drinking trough, where the words would not be washed away, Jane printed a short message which said, "Sylvie, we have gone with the Savashun Army.

Joe, Jane, Rufus."

"There," she said with satisfaction. "She surely won'
miss that."

Then the horse had a drink and they all had a drink, and
now they were ready. Up they all climbed and clup, clup,
down Main Street past the Green to the good hard dirt
road that led to Shingle Hill.

The man kept right on sleeping. You would think that
bumping over the little wooden bridge at the foot of Shingle
Hill would awaken him. But no. He didn't even stir.

Up Shingle Hill in a horse and wagon! Many were the
times they had plodded wearily up that steep hill on foot
to pick violets, or goldenrod and asters. Now up, up the
horse drew the light wagon and the three children and the
sleeping man. Janey looked at the man, his head on a pile
of newspapers. Yes, he was still asleep. And from time to
time he snored, much to everybody's delight. The children
began to sing. How far behind them now were Main Street,
Sunday School, pot roast and onions. Up, up, up Shingle
Hill.

Rufus and Jane had to hang on tight as they slowly
climbed the steep grade.

Joe yelled to them, "If the road gets too steep and the horse stops, you'll have to jump off quick, get a big rock, and put it under the wheel so we won't slide back down the hill."

"Right," said Rufus, "I've seen it done."

But there was no need for emergency measures. The horse was young and strong, and with a slow, steady pace he pulled them all over the brow of the hill. Here Joe drew up at the side of the road. The horse started eating branches off a crab-apple tree.

The Salvation Army man slept on. But the children jumped down, stretched their legs, and looked at the view. Way off through the trees they could see the white spire of Peter Frost's church on the Green. The flag-pole too. Farther on, the sun caught the sparkle of the water of the harbor, and way off on the other side of the harbor they could just make out the slumbering form of the Sleeping Giant—three round hills, lying close together and resembling a huge being resting under a mantle of green trees.

After a few moments Janey said, "We better be going or we'll get the minister here late to the revival meeting."

"Minister!" ejaculated Rufus. "He's not a minister, is

he?"

"Well, sort of. And see, he has Captain on his hat."

"Captain!" repeated Rufus with awe in his voice. "We better take good care of him."

"Well, Captain or no Captain, I wish he had fallen asleep on the newspapers in the back of the wagon, so we could all sit in front," said Jane.

The three looked at the man, but snores were their only answer.

There was beginning to be something exasperating about those snores. "Hey, Captain," yelled Janey.

But the Captain slept on.

"The drum!" said Rufus, reaching for it and sounding a deafening tattoo on it.

Sure enough! The drum did it. The man leaped out of his seat to the ground. He started to wave his arms and talk. Recovering, he looked about him in amazement.

"Is this Orchard Grove?" he asked incredulously, "or where are we anyway?"

Joe pointed to a sign on the crab-apple tree.

"No, sir," he said, "but don't worry. Orchard Grove's only a couple of miles away. We are going to take you

86

there. Wouldn't you be more comfortable resting on the piles of papers in back?"

The man yawned and stretched. "You're right. I might be," he answered. He lifted an oilcloth curtain that hung there to keep draughts from the back of his neck when he

was driving and crawled into the covered part of the wagon. He fell asleep on a pile of newspapers before Joe, Jane, and Rufus even had time to say Giddyap to the horse.

Suddenly their road was blocked by a sign:

Road closed—Detour

"Detour!" said Joe. "Which road, I wonder. Wouldn't you think they'd tell you which one goes to Orchard Grove?"

There were two possible roads to take, with little to distinguish between them.

"I vote on the lower road," said Jane. "It looks as though it's going in about the same direction as the one we're on."

"Yes," agreed Rufus. "That other road looks like it's nothing but an old cow path."

"All right. We'll take the lower one then," agreed Joe. "If it's wrong, we can turn around and come back."

"Hup-hup," said Joe to the horse.

The horse started with a lurch. He swung onto the side road too rapidly. As the wagon turned, the back wheels skidded into the ditch on the side of the road.

"Hey!" cried Jane as she was jolted from her seat to the floor of the wagon.

Joe braced his feet against the floor and called words of encouragement to the horse, "All right, Billy. Hup-hup, Billy," he said.

The horse pulled and strained but the wagon wheels just churned around in the dirt.

"Come on, Billy, come on," the children encouraged.

The horse gave a mighty pull and with a creak and a groan the wagon lurched out of the ditch.

"Phew!" said Joe, mopping his brow. "Narrow escape!"

Jane readjusted herself on the seat next to Joe. "Ouch," she said, rubbing her knees that she had bruised in falling.

Rufus clapped his hands. "Giddyap," he said. The horse burst into a fine gallop jouncing the wagon over ruts in care-free fashion.

Joe, Jane, and Rufus didn't look back. None of them looked back once on the scene of their near disaster. If they had, they might have seen the Captain sprawled on the ground along with piles of newspapers. That last lurch out of the ditch had sent him flying out of the wagon into the ditch. Yes, there he was, leaning on his elbows and cupping his mouth with his hands as he called, "Come back. Come back!"

He was wide awake now all right and he called with all his might. "Come back, I say!"

He might as well be shout-ing to himself, though. How

could the Moffats hear him above the clatter of the horse's hooves and the wagon wheels? They couldn't, of course, and the next minute they had disappeared altogether around the bend in the road.

The children didn't notice that the Captain was gone and they didn't notice the dark clouds that were gathering overhead. Or the way the wind had begun to whistle in the trees and how the leaves were turning their backs to the wind, as though preparing to fend off a blow. They were too engrossed with the exciting business of driving a real horse and wagon to notice these signs.

But the horse knew a storm was coming. He twitched his ears. He lowered and raised his head uneasily. Finally he let out a deep neigh that echoed through the woods.

"What's the matter?" asked Rufus.

As if to answer him, an ear-splitting clap of thunder rent the air. The horse reared up on his hind legs a moment and then down the road he tore.

Joe clung tightly to the reins. Janey and Rufus crouched on the floor.

"Orchard Grove ought to be around the next corner. Don't be scared," Joe shouted above the storm.

Orchard Grove wasn't around the next corner. But a welcome sight did meet their eyes. And what a surprise, considering they were expecting Orchard Grove! Instead there was old Natby's blacksmith shop at the end of Elm Street. This road they had taken had led right around town in a circle. The horse galloped into the shed and came snorting to a stop just as the heavens opened and let down such a rain as had not fallen before that summer. The wind tore branches from the trees. The thunder cracked like a giant whip and lightning sizzled through the air.

"Phew!" said Joe. "What luck to find a shelter!"

"Where do you suppose old Natby is?" asked Rufus.

"Probably at church," said Jane.

"What will the Captain say when he wakes up and finds we're just as far from Orchard Grove as when we started?" asked Joey uneasily.

"He won't wake unless we beat the drum," screamed Jane above the thunder. "Imagine sleeping through this storm."

"Well, anyway, he'll be pleased we found this shelter for his horse. Besides, how could he hold a revival meeting in the rain?" Joe comforted himself.

"To think we just went around in a circle!" marveled Jane.

"Yes. The Green is only five minutes away. I should-a

known better too," said Joe, rather ashamed. "All the times I been biking up there with Chet Pudge."

"Well, things look different behind a horse," said Jane consolingly.

They sat there in the broad doorway of the blacksmith shop waiting until the worst of the storm should be over.

They were impatient to be off.

"Rain, rain, go away," chanted Janey, watching the drops falling through the leaves.

At last the rain began to abate.

"Let's go now," said Joe. "And I s'pose we better go back to the Green and take the Shore road to Orchard Grove. These country roads will be terrible after this rain."

"Right," agreed Janey and Rufus.

So back to the Green then. The horse neighed. He was glad to be on the move again. The quick summer storm had spent itself and already the sun was breaking through the heavy clouds.

They trotted down Elm Street. Now, clop, clop-a, cloppity clop-a to Main Street, and here they were approaching the Green. The Green looked most welcome to them. To tell the truth they were all getting tired and they wished to goodness that they might bid the Captain good-by and get home to Sunday dinner, to Robinson Crusoe, to paper dolls. There came a moment of complete silence as they thought of these things. The silence made Janey remark, "You know what?"

"What?" asked Rufus sleepily. The cloppity clop-a was

94

making him drowsy.

"Well, when we were going out of town the Captain snored and snored. He hasn't snored for ever so long. S'funny."

"People don't snore every minute," said Joe testily.

"No, but I think this man either snores or he's awake. He's certainly not snoring and I'm sure we'd hear him if he were awake. I don't think he's there," Jane announced solemnly.

A deep silence greeted this observation of Jane's. Then Joe said still more testily, "Jane, you often think of troublesome things." Then he added a little less crossly, "How could he *not* be there? We haven't seen him get out. But just to please you, we'll look."

He handed the reins to Jane. Then he lifted the heavy oilcloth curtain and he looked. They all looked. They turned their heads back to the street again. Joe took up the reins, spat out of the side of the wagon as he had seen certain people do, and said, "Gone!"

The Captain lost! Out of his own horse and wagon! Phew!

No wonder they all looked pretty subdued as they drew

up at the drinking trough. No doubt ordinarily looking for the Captain would have seemed like sport to them. What? Look for a lost Captain? Sure! What fun! That's what they ordinarily would have thought. But having lost the Captain of the Salvation Army out of his own horse and wagon was a song of a different tune. Moreover they were tired— worn out, in fact, by everything that had happened. First they had lost the road. Now they had lost the Captain. Well, they would just have to turn around and find him.

They jumped down to stretch their legs for a moment before beginning the search. They scarcely noticed Mrs. Shoemaker who had spread the Sunday *Register* on a bench and was sitting on it so she wouldn't get wet. They sat down beside her and tried to think what they should do. Mrs. Shoemaker listened to their conversation and she kept exclaiming, "Well, I never! Lost the Captain of the Salvation Army! Well, I never!" The children felt they could think a whole lot better if Mrs. Shoemaker would only stop this "Well, I never" business. They had an important question to decide. Since they had gone around a complete circle, should they go back the way they had just come? Or should they go back the way they had driven in the first place?

To make matters worse, they noticed that all the message they had written on the drinking trough had been washed away by the rain except for the words "Army" and "Joe." This meant that Mama would be worrying too.

At this moment Sylvie ran across the street from the Town Hall.

"Hi!" she cried. "There you are! Mama wants you to come home. She sent me to look for you. Where have you been anyway? What did you mean by 'Army'?" she asked, pointing to the message on the drinking trough. "I thought it might have some connection with that sign over there," she added, indicating a large poster in front of the Town Hall which said:

JOIN THE ARMY—ENLIST!

They all laughed at the idea of Sylvie thinking they might have joined the army and while they were explaining what really had happened, who should come along but the Reverend Mr. Gandy! What a crowd was there, and more and more coming. Everyone making proposals and supposing this and supposing that, and suggesting this and suggesting that! Joey, Janey, and Rufus began to feel important in spite of themselves. They began to feel as though they were a rescue party.

"Come on, kids," said Joe. "We better start on the expedition."

They rose from the bench and were about to mount the wagon again when, look! Who was that hurrying across Main Street? Yes, of course. Mama! Mama in her black gloves and hat with the violets.

"Well, well," she said. "What's going on? Why don't you come home and eat your dinner?"

"We can't, Mama," said Rufus solemnly.

"Can't!" echoed Mama, amazed.

"No," sighed Joe. "We lost the Captain of the Salvation Army."

"And now we've got to find him," said Jane sadly.

"And take him to the revival meeting like we said we would," said Joe.

"Well . . . tell me about it," said Mama.

Now that Mama was on the scene the children felt more like talking. They kept interrupting one another all the

time. "All right, Jane, now you told enough. Let me talk now." Or, "But *I* want to tell about the blacksmith shop." They became so excited, talking and jumping around, they didn't pay any attention to the funny-looking man who was coming across the Green. Mrs. Shoemaker was the first to notice him.

"I declare," she whispered to Mr. Gandy, nudging him in the ribs. "Don't you see the strange-looking people

in town now that the new Second Avenue trolley line has been opened?"

"All men are our brothers, strange-looking or otherwise, Mrs. Shoemaker," said the Reverend Mr. Gandy.

As the stranger drew nearer he didn't seem so much odd-looking as he did just plain wet. He joined the group and said,

"Almost enough people here to hold a meeting." And whistling, he went over to stroke his horse's nose.

"It's the Captain," screamed Jane. "My—how wet!"

"Oh, the Captain," exclaimed all the others, standing up.

"Aye. Captain Rowley of the Salvation Army," said he. "At your service," said he, giving Joe a meaning look.

Joe was so covered with confusion he could say nothing. Jane came to his rescue and said, "I guess you thought you'd wake up in Orchard Grove. I'm very sorry. If you hadn't gotten out of the wagon, you might have . . . finally . . ."

"Hadn't gotten out!" exploded the Captain. "Hadn't gotten out indeed!" Then to everyone's amazement he described how he had been thrown from the wagon. " 'Come back!' I yelled. I might as well have saved my breath though, for all the good it did," he said, glowering at the three, who were naturally speechless at his story.

"Well, I never!" said Mrs. Shoemaker.

When the Captain had finally finished telling what had happened to him and had listened to what had happened to them, he said, "Well, I guess there's no use my going to Orchard Grove now at all. Meeting will be over and Captain Rowley will not have been there like he said he would," he said sadly.

"Oh, oh, . . . I'm sorry," Joe said apologetically. But now Mama interrupted and said the whole party must come home to the yellow house and have Sunday dinner. "You too, Mrs. Shoemaker," she said cordially.

Mrs. Shoemaker hesitated a moment. Then she said ruefully, "Thank you, but I have had my dinner, so I'll be on my way, I guess. I'm meeting Mrs. Cadwalader in the cemetery. You know, we spend every Sunday afternoon in the cemetery. It's so restful."

So she moved on up the street. When she turned around at the corner, she was most surprised to see Mr. Gandy helping Mama up to the driver's seat next to the Captain. Sylvie and the rest of them walked slowly behind, except for Rufus who was too tired to walk and sat up on the newspapers in the back.

"Mind you hang on," said the Captain, giving him a solemn wink as they started.

Rufus found the drum and banged it good and hard Mama turned around and said, "Hush, it's Sunday," and then to the horse, she said briskly, "Giddyap, giddyap, sir."

"Gee, he goes as good for her as for us," said Joe to Jane.

"Sure, why not?" she answered.

5

THE GHOST IN THE ATTIC

JANE CAME SKIPPING UP THE STREET. WHAT A GOOD DAY it had been so far! And it was going to be even better, of that she was sure. It had been a good day in school because the drawing teacher, Miss Partridge, who visited every class in town once in the fall, once in the winter, and once in the spring, had paid her autumn visit that day.

Everyone in Jane's class had drawn an autumn leaf. Everyone in Rufus' a pumpkin. Everyone in Joe's an apple. All the children in the grammar schools came home with

Louis Slobodkin

a drawing fluttering in the wind—a drawing of a pumpkin, an apple, or an autumn leaf. It is true that sometimes the children grew tired of drawing leaves, pumpkins, and apples. However, Miss Partridge never thought of letting them draw anything else.

Still, no matter what they had to draw, the children loved the day of Miss Partridge's visit: first, because all studies would be swept aside for the sake of autumn leaves and pumpkins; secondly, because Miss Partridge was so amiable. She was always smiling, always. The children called her the smiley teacher. No one had ever seen her frown or heard her speak a cross word. Not a bit like Mr. Allgood, the music master, who was so strict he set every heart pounding like a blacksmith's hammer the minute he came in the door. Why, when Mr. Allgood entered the room, the children, without being told one word, automatically sat up in their chairs so straight that their backs would ache for the rest of the day. Chet Pudge stopped putting Jane's braids in the ink-well. Edie Ellenbach stuck her chewing gum under the seat lest she be asked to sing her music slip alone. Mr. Allgood knew the minute you opened your mouth if there was anything in it. Even Peter

Frost would toe the mark and stop making slingshot bullets out of his arithmetic paper. Certainly Mr. Allgood, whom all the children called Mr. Allbad (only out of school, way in the distance), was a figure to be reckoned with.

And if it came to a toss-up, who would you rather have visit the class, Mr. Allgood or Miss Partridge? Why, Miss Partridge easily walked away with all the votes. She always said "Good! Good!" to you about your drawing, whereas your singing seemed to put Mr. Allgood in a fearful temper.

Well, so that was the kind of day it had been. A visit from the smiley teacher! There had been no sitting up straight as ramrods for her. More sticks of gum than ever were stuck in the children's mouths and oh! what a bad day it had been for Janey's braids! To cap the climax, as soon as the drawing lesson was over and the best autumn leaf drawings had been placed around the room on exhibition, Miss Partridge had produced thirty-eight orange lollipops, one for everyone in the class, and said that now they would play games, have stories, and go home fifteen minutes early.

Why all these good things in one day?

Because today was Halloween!

Jane shivered as she thought of the stories Miss Partridge had told with the shades lowered. One about a golden arm; one dreadful one about stairs and something creeping up them; and one about "my grandfather, Henry Watty" that was the most scary of all. Then they'd played some good rough games and left early.

Janey scuffled through the dry crackling leaves in the gutter, holding her drawing carefully in one hand for Mama She felt so excited about Halloween she forgot to breathe the prayer, "Dear God, please don't let anyone buy the yellow house," which the sight of the For Sale sign usually brought to her lips. She skipped through the gate, skipped as fast as she could around the house to the back door with Catherine-the-cat racing after her. She burst into the kitchen that today smelled of hot gingerbread and ran into the Grape Room where Mrs. Shoemaker was trying on a very tight white satin gown.

Mama's mouth was full of pins, but she stopped pulling the gown down over Mrs. Shoemaker's fuzzy yellow hair long enough to look admiringly at the drawing of the autumn leaf. It would be put away later with all the apples, pumpkins, and autumn leaves in the box where Mama kept these things. She nodded her head up and down when Jane said, "May I have a piece of gingerbread?"

Jane grabbed the gingerbread and ran out to join Rufus and Joe in the barn.

"Are you gettin' ready for tonight?" she asked.

"You bet," said Joe. "Sylvie said to make a ghost. We're goin' to put her in the attic an' scare Peter Frost."

"When?"

"Tonight."

Jane sucked her breath in between her teeth. Ooh! Think of a ghost in the attic!

"Are you sure Peter Frost will come?"

"Oh, sure," said Joe. "He said to me, 'Ghosts! Ha-ha! Ghosts! No such thing!' And I said to him, 'Sure, in our attic there's a ghost.' "

"What did he say to that?" asked Jane.

"He said, 'Ghost, nothin'!' "

"And what did you say then?"

"I said, 'All right, if you don't believe me, come on over to our house at eight o'clock' and we'd show him."

"Well, we better get busy," said Rufus energetically. 'What do we do first?"

"First we have to carve the head. This ghost is going to have a pumpkin head." Joe went to a dark corner of the barn and fetched a beautiful pumpkin head. The three of them set to work digging out a most startling face. And as they worked, they reviewed their grudges against Peter Frost. There were plenty of them. It was high time something should be done to even the score.

"Remember that time he made Rufus fall off the hitchin post?"

"Remember that time he told Jane to put her mouth up against the hole in the fence and he would give her a piece of candy and he gave her a mouthful of sand instead?"

"Remember how he always is pullin' Sylvie's curls every chance he gets? And hard—so it hurts."

"Remember that time he almost got Jane arrested and she had to hide in the bread-box?"

Remember? Indeed they remembered all these insults

and a great many others besides. Something just had to be done to settle the account. They worked harder and faster than they'd ever worked before.

After a while Rufus said, "I know what. We can use my teeth in this head."

"Oh, fine," said Joe. "Where are they?"

Without answering, Rufus climbed to the loft. He found the secret hiding-place under the beams where he kept some of his treasures. Here was the old tin Prince Albert tobacco box where he kept his collection of teeth. Safe apparently and quite full too. He looked at them lovingly. Some of the teeth were quite small. These were Rufus' own. But most of the collection he had found under the Grape Room window. Dr. Witty, who had lived in the yellow house before the Moffats, was a dentist. Apparently every time he pulled out a tooth, he had just tossed it out of the window. The first tooth Rufus had found one day when he was digging a hole, hoping to get a peep into China. It had filled him with the most amazed delight. In excitement he had rushed in to show it to Mama, thinking she would be as interested as he was. On the contrary, she hadn't been at all pleased about it and had said, "Throw that nasty thing away." He didn't show her his finds after that, but stored them privately in his Prince Albert box.

"Well, what are you doin' up there?" called Jane.

"Comin'," said Rufus, carefully putting them back in the box. Making his way down the ladder, he poured them out between Jane and Joe.

They looked at the teeth admiringly.

"Gee, those are swell," said Jane. "Look at that one, will you?" she said, pointing to an enormous one.

"Yeh," agreed Rufus, looking at it with pride. "Old Natby the blacksmith gave me that one. He said he'd been shoein' an old mare one day and that tooth fell out of her mouth. He said it was the biggest he'd ever seen."

They stuck the

teeth in the pumpkin head and at last it was finished. They looked at their work with satisfaction. Phew! She looked gruesome, particularly with that old mare's tooth hanging over her lower lip. Twilight was approaching and they had difficulty in seeing clearly. As it grew darker, they automatically lowered their voices. Now they were talking in whispers, putting the finishing touches on their plan for the night. They began to feel a creepy uneasiness. Their own ideas scared them and sent prickles up and down their spines. They jumped when Sylvie came to the kitchen door and called them to supper, and then tore from the barn as though all the hobyahs, pookas, and goblins in the world were at their heels.

The light from the kitchen spread a warm welcome to them. From up and down the street they could hear the different whistles and calls that summoned the other children in the block home to their dinners. Pookas, hobyahs, and goblins fled . . . temporarily. The five Moffats sat down around the kitchen table. As they ate, the oil lamp in the middle of the table sputtered and sent little curls of black smoke to the top of the glass chimney.

"A wind is rising," said Mama.

The children exchanged pleased glances. A wind! So much the better.

Jane whispered to Sylvie, "Have you had a chance to bring the Madame upstairs?" For Madame-the-bust was to be the ghost this night.

"Not yet," Sylvie whispered back. "There's plenty of time."

"Plenty of time!" echoed Jane impatiently. "Supposin' Peter Frost comes before everything's ready?" She couldn't eat another bite. Rufus had finished too. Finally the others put down their spoons. Dinner was over.

"Now," said Mama, "I see no reason, even if it is Halloween, why I shouldn't leave you four children. Mrs. Pudge wants me to talk over plans for her silver wedding anniversary dress, so I think I'll go tonight. Now don't be gallivanting through the streets after eight o'clock. And, Joey, please tie the garbage pail to the back porch or some of those street hoodlums will be trying to tie it to the lamp post. And see that the rake and anything else that's movable is locked in the barn. I won't be very late." Then she put on the black velvet hat with the blue violets that matched her eyes and went out.

How still and empty the house suddenly became without Mama in it! Inside not a sound except the ticking of the clock in the sitting-room and the creaking of the cane rocking-chair that no one was sitting in. Outside the wind rustled in the trees and a dog that sounded miles away howled mournfully. The children sat hushed and motionless. Suddenly a hot coal fell in the grate. Catherine-the-cat jumped from her place under the stove, arched her back, and bristled her tail. The children broke into screams of laughter and the house became friendly again.

"Well," said Sylvie, "we'd better hurry. First the pumpkin. Who'll get that?"

Who indeed? Who would go out in that dark barn and get the pumpkin head? No one answered, so Joe and Jane were sent.

"We'll stand in the door," said Sylvie.

Breathlessly, Joe and Jane tore to the barn, snatched up the fierce-looking pumpkin head, and tore back into the warm kitchen.

"Now the Madame," said Sylvie, solemnly lighting the smallest oil lamp and leading the way into the Grape Room. Catherine-the-cat leaped ahead of her, wagging her tail restlessly. What was the matter with Catherine tonight, anyway? She kept meowing and meowing and following them all around. Sylvie set the lamp carefully on the table. Catherine-the-cat sat in the shadow. Her yellow eyes shone with a knowing gleam.

"Look at Catherine," said Jane. "She's watchin' us and watchin' us."

"Let her watch," said Sylvie as she carefully removed Mrs. Shoemaker's white satin gown from Madame-the-bust. Then she grasped Madame tightly in her arms.

"You carry the pumpkin, Joe. And Rufus, you bring your scooter. Jane can carry the sheets."

Slowly the procession made its way out of the Grape Room, into the hall, up the stairs to the second floor. Joe led the way with his pocket flashlight. From the hall upstairs, a stepladder led to the attic which did not have a regular door but a hatch which Joe had to push up with his shoulders. It fell open with a groan and the strange musty smell of the attic greeted them. Joe set the head on the floor and flashed the light down the stepladder so the others could see to climb up.

Sylvie hoisted Madame up before her and climbed in.

Then Rufus handed up his scooter and hoisted himself in. As Jane was making her way up, Catherine-the-cat leaped past her and disappeared into the dark recesses of the attic. Jane bit her tongue but managed to keep from screaming. That cat! She was always doing unexpected things behind you.

The four Moffats stood around the entrance, the nearest point to the kitchen, to safety. Joe's tiny flashlight scarcely penetrated the darkness of the attic. But they knew what was up here all right without seeing. Dr. Witty had had many different hobbies. Collecting and stuffing wild animals and birds was one of them. He stored these in the attic in the yellow house. In one corner was a stuffed owl. In another, a stuffed wildcat. And all around were a great many little stuffed partridges and quail. The four children shivered, partly from cold, partly from excitement.

"Oh, let's hurry and get out of this place," said Jane.

They placed the scooter in the corner by the owl. Then they put Madame on the scooter, put the pumpkin head with its ominous, gaping mouth on her headless neck, and draped the sheets about her. They tied one end of the rope to the scooter and made a loop in the other end in order to be able to pull the ghost around easily. The end of the rope with the loop they placed near the hatchway.

"All right," said Sylvie. "Now let's see how she looks."

They went to the head of the ladder. Joe flashed his light on Madame—Madame-the-bust no longer, or Mrs. Shoemaker or Miss Nippon either, but Madame-the-ghost!

"Phew!" he whistled.

"Boy, oh, boy!" said Rufus.

"Oh," shivered Jane, "come on."

As fast as they could, they pushed the hatch back in place and hurried helter-skelter to the kitchen where they warmed their hands over the kitchen fire.

"Boy, oh, boy!" said Rufus again, "what a ghost!"

Then they all put on the most fearful masks that Sylvie had made for them. And just in the nick of time too, for here was Peter Frost stamping on the back porch.

"Hey there, Moffats," he said witheringly. "Where's your old ghost then?"

Oh, his arrogance was insufferable.

"Don't worry," said Sylvie, "you'll see her all right. But you must be quiet."

"Haw-haw," jeered Peter Frost.

But he stopped short, for out of the night came a long-drawn howl, a howl of reproach.

Sylvie, Joe, Jane, and Rufus had the same thought. Catherine-the-cat! They had forgotten her up there with the ghost. But Peter Frost! Why, he knew nothing of that of course, and although he was inclined to toss the matter lightly aside, still he blanched visibly when again from some mysterious dark recess of the house came the same wild howl.

The four Moffats knew when to be silent and they were silent now. So was Peter Frost. So was the whole house. It was so silent it began to speak with a thousand voices. When Mama's rocking-chair creaked, Peter Frost looked at it as though he expected to see the ghost sitting right in it. Somewhere a shutter came unfastened and banged against the house with persistent regularity. The clock in the sitting-room ticked slowly, painfully, as though it had a lump in its throat; then stopped altogether. Even the Moffats began to feel scared, particularly Rufus. He began to think this whole business on a par with G-R-I-N-D your bones in "Jack and the Beanstalk."

Peter Frost swallowed his breath with a great gulp and said in a voice a trifle less jeering, "Well, what're we waitin' for? I want to see yer old ghost."

"Very well, then," said the four Moffats in solemn voices. "Follow us."

Again they left the warm safety of the kitchen, mounted the inky black stairs to the second floor, each one holding to the belt of the one in front. When they reached the stepladder, they paused a moment to count heads.

"Aw, you don't think I'm gonna skin out without seeing your silly old ghost, do yer?" asked Peter Frost. However, blustering though his words were, there could be no doubt that his hand, the one that held onto Joe's belt, was shaking and shaking.

"Now we go up the stepladder," said Joe in a hoarse whisper. "I'll push open the hatch."

Cautiously the five mounted the stepladder. It seemed to lead to a never-ending pit of darkness.

"Why don't you light your flash?" asked Peter Frost, doing his best to sound carefree and easy.

"And scare away the ghost, I suppose," snorted Joe. "You know, a ghost isn't comin' out where there's a light and all this many people. That is, unless there's a certain one around it happens to be interested in."

Another howl interrupted Joe's words. This sounded so close to them now that the four Moffats were afraid Peter Frost would recognize the voice of Catherine-the-cat. But he didn't. He began to shake and shake more violently than ever, making the stepladder they were standing on shiver and creak.

Joe pushed the trap door up with his shoulders. It fell open with a groan just as it had done before. They all climbed in and stood on the attic floor. Except for a pale glow from the light below, the attic was in the thickest blackness. For a moment they stood there in silence. Then suddenly Joe gave a swift flash into the corner of the attic. It fell for a second on the stuffed wildcat.

Peter Frost started but said not a word.

Then swiftly Joe flashed the light in the other corner. The stuffed owl stared at them broodingly.

But Peter Frost said nothing.

And then Joe flashed his light on Madame-the-ghost, herself. There she was, lurking in the corner, her orange head gaping horribly. All the children gasped, but still

Peter Frost said nothing. All of a sudden, without any warning whatsoever, Madame-the-ghost started careening madly toward them. And dragging heavy chains behind her too, from the sound.

Jane called out in a shrill voice:

"Peter Frost! Peter Frost!
E-e-e-e-e-e-e-e-e!"

Joe flashed his light on and off rapidly. Madame-the-ghost dashed wildly round and round the attic. The same howl rent the air! The shutters banged. Then Peter Frost let out a roar of terror. That THING was after HIM. He tore around the attic room, roaring like a bull. And the ghost, dragging its horrible chains, tore after him.

"Let me go," he bellowed. But he couldn't find the hatch. Around the attic and around the attic he stumbled, kicking over stuffed partridges and quail. Finally he tripped over the wildcat and sprawled on the floor. Joe flashed his light on them for a second and when Peter Frost saw that he was sitting on the wildcat, he let out another piercing yell and leaped to his feet. He had seen now where the hatch was and he meant to escape before that ghost could catch up

with him. Again he tripped and was down once more, this time with the ghost right on top of him. She would smother him with those ghastly robes of hers.

"She's got me! She's got me!" he roared.

Frantically he shook himself free of the ghost, and in wild leaps he made again for the hatch.

But now Rufus and Jane too had stood all they could of this nerve-racking business. They both began howling with fright and screaming, "Mama, Mama!" What with Peter Frost's yelling, Catherine-the-cat's yowling, the screams of Rufus and Jane, Sylvie herself began laughing hysterically and the place sounded like bedlam. To make matters worse, the battery of Joe's flashlight gave out, so there was no way of turning on the blessed light and showing everyone there was no real ghost.

No, the ghost was real enough to Peter Frost, and as he finally reached the hatch and clattered down the stairs he thought he could still feel its cold breath on his neck and cheeks. The four Moffats followed after him, half tumbling, half sliding, until they reached the kitchen. Peter Frost tore out the back door with a bang and left the four of them there in the kitchen, breathless and sobbing and laughing all at once.

"Phew," gasped Joe. "Some ghost, I'll say!"

" 'Twas real then?" said Rufus, getting ready to howl again.

"Of course not, silly," said Joe, whose courage had returned. "Come on, though. We've got to get the things down. Mama'll be home in a minute. Sylvie better carry the little lamp."

Rufus and Jane did not want to go back into that attic. They'd had enough of ghosts and goblins. But neither did they want to stay down in the kitchen alone. So up to the attic the four went once more. And with all the light made from the little lamp Rufus could see there wasn't any real ghost at all. Just Madame and the pumpkin head he'd stuck his own teeth into and his own scooter that Catherine-the-cat, caught in the loop of the rope, was dragging around and around.

Swiftly Sylvie unloosened the cat. She gave them all a triumphant leer and leaped down the hatch with short meows. Next they dismantled the ghost and returned Madame to the Grape Room where Sylvie dressed her again in Mrs. Shoemaker's new dress. The pumpkin head had received many bad cracks, but they put it in the sitting-room window with a candle lighted inside of it, where it looked quite jolly and altogether harmless.

Then they sat down to talk the evening over. They agreed the ghost had been a success.

"That'll teach him to be always tormentin' the life outta us," said Jane with a yawn.

"Sh-h-h," warned Sylvie. "Here comes Mama."

Mama came in the door. She took off her hat and wiped

the tears that the wind had put there from her eyes.

"Goodness," she said. "The witches certainly must be out tonight all right enough. I just passed Peter Frost racing like sixty up the street. He muttered some gibberish about a ghost being after him. And look at Catherine! She looks as though she's preparing for a wild night. And why, for goodness' sakes! Will you look here, please?" Mama's voice went on from the Grape Room where she had gone to hang her hat. "Just look here! Mrs. Shoemaker's dress is turned completely around. The hobgoblins must have done it." (Here Rufus smothered his laughter in his brown chubby fist.) "Well, well . . ." she continued, "let's bob for apples . . ."

6

THE SAILOR'S HORNPIPE

THE MOFFATS ALL WENT TO MISS CHICHESTER'S DANCING
school in Moose Hall. They didn't have to pay Miss Chichester a penny for their lessons. Mama did a great deal of
sewing for Miss Chichester and she was not always able to
settle her bills with Mama. Mama said they should strike a
bargain. The way Miss Chichester might settle her bills
was to give all the Moffats dancing lessons free. Or rather,

all except Rufus. Rufus would go as soon as he was a little older. Although, for that matter, as far as age went he really could go now. Hughie Pudge was in the dancing class and he was only six, just a few months older than Rufus. But he and Rufus always got into a dispute which ended in a big fight. Or else they spent their time firing spitballs from their slingshots at the moose heads at each end of the hall. Naturally these doings upset the class. One or the other, therefore, must be kept out. Since Rufus did not pay for his lessons and Hughie did, of course Rufus was the one Miss Chichester felt she would have to get along without. Rufus did not mind in the least being deprived of dancing lessons. He much preferred playing marbles or riding his scooter.

Of the three Moffats, Sylvie, Joe and Jane, who did go to Miss Chichester's dancing school, Sylvie was the only one who loved it wholeheartedly. She was very quick and graceful. Dancing came as naturally to her as breathing. It was no wonder Miss Chichester made her do half the teaching.

As for Jane, she loved the thought of dancing school, but when she got there how different it always was from what she had imagined! Before going to sleep at night, Jane pictured herself dancing as beautifully and gracefully as Sylvie. Now she would have the center of the floor at dancing school, spinning lightly as a leaf, while all the others held their breath. Or she would be leading the Virginia Reel with the greatest of ease and assurance. Her arms and legs would behave perfectly. But, in real life, her arms and legs acted as though they were stuffed with lead. And her hands and feet seemed to swell to extraordinary proportions.

Moreover, on dancing school days Mama always did her hair up in curlers. Instead of her two familiar pigtails, strange long curls bobbed behind her, distracting her attention. They looked absolutely ridiculous, she was sure. "Corkscrews!" Peter Frost called them.

As far as she was concerned, the only really nice thing about dancing school was the slippers with the pom-poms on their toes and the ribbon lacings that wound halfway up her white-stockinged legs. Even though she never could dance at dancing school the way she could in her dreams, the slippers alone made it worth while.

But Joe now! Joe hated dancing school and didn't have even the consolation of pom-poms on his slippers. He hated dancing school and he was no good at it. He was good at lots of other things. He was good at spinning tops. He could fly kites better than anybody else on the block. He always had a good pencil with a fine sharp point in his pocket. He could whistle and he could whittle. Yes, all these things he was good at, but he was not good at dancing school and he did not like it. Not at all. He begged Mama not to make him go.

"I'll rake the leaves, shovel the snow, mow the lawn, sift the ashes, without your ever even askin' me to," he said to Mama.

But Mama said he should go. If he didn't go, Miss Chichester would feel very badly. She would feel as though she were not keeping her part of the bargain. "But I think I feel worse going to dancing school than Miss Chichester would if I didn't go," Joe said miserably. He knew though that remonstrance was useless. Mama knew he didn't like parties, dancing school, speaking pieces. Still she thought he should do these things. "You must learn to be graceful and to have nice manners even though you are a boy," she said. To Mama this business exchange of dancing for sewing seemed a heaven-sent opportunity. How otherwise could she possibly afford to give her children the advantages of dancing school? Under the circumstances, she thought Joe should go. "Try to like it," she pleaded with him.

Well, since it seemed so important to Mama, Joe went. But he often hid behind the piano at dancing school, particularly during the Tom Joneses and the Virginia Reels, which he never could do without getting mixed up.

Sometimes if luck were with him, he was able to pass nearly the whole hour behind the piano very pleasantly indeed with an apple or a book. And he would not have to listen to Miss Chichester call to Miss Nippon and tell her to repeat "Shine, little glow-worm, glimmer, glimmer," because he, Joe, had gotten himself and his partner and most of his immediate neighbors hopelessly out of step.

Joe always waked up in the morning of these dancing school days with a funny feeling in the pit of his stomach. What was it? He'd lie there in bed for a minute or two, wondering. He'd done his geography and his spelling and he'd even gone ahead a chapter in history. Then he'd remember. "O' course," he'd sigh, "it's dancin' school today."

And the worst day of all for him was the one when Miss Chichester gave her recital. He hadn't expected the day to be bad at all. In fact he had expected this day to be easier to endure than the ordinary dancing school days because Miss Chichester had said to him, "All you will have to do, Joe, is to usher the guests into their seats. I'll help you see that the important people have the best seats in the front row. After that you can turn pages for Miss Nippon."

So that was the plan. Joe must stand by the piano, hair brushed neatly aside, toes out, and in his best Sunday suit of dark brown corduroy. Whenever Miss Nippon whispered, "Turn," he was to turn the page of her music. This seemed rather silly to Joe. Miss Nippon appeared perfectly capable of turning her music for herself every other day. In fact the entire class had learned to pause, sometimes with one foot suspended in the air, while Miss Nippon fumbled with the page. Why put on these lugs?

However, all this was far more to his taste than to dance

the sailor's hornpipe. Phew! That is what he was first sched-
uled to do. Dance the sailor's hornpipe! But he had such
difficulty learning the steps, Miss Chichester finally said
that Chet Pudge would have to do it instead. Even though
Chet was very fat and grew very red in the face and puffy,
he would have to dance the sailor's hornpipe. And instead,
Joe could do the ushering and the turning of the pages and
get ten cents besides if all turned out well.

So is it any wonder that Joe looked forward to the day of
the recital as one dancing school
day, anyway, when he would be
free of all care and worry? And he
watched Jane and Sylvie practice
their dances around the house with
an air of compassion.

Joe may have been carefree about
the recital. But Jane wasn't. She
had to dance "To a Wild Rose"
with Letitia Murdock. How would
they carry it off, she wondered?
She, Jane, did it pretty well all by
herself in the lilac bush. But when

she and Letitia stood up there in Moose Hall before all those people, how would it go then? So far, in all the rehearsals, she and Letitia finished the dance long before Miss Nippon finished the music. That was not right. Dance and music were supposed to end at the same moment.

And she worried about her hair, too. There was no chance of Mama letting her wear her everyday braids. No, a recital was a special occasion and would require curls. If it rained, the curls would come out. Jane prayed for a clear sunny day for the recital. She said all the charms she knew to avert rain and prayed to God to send a clear day. Rufus generously did the same as a favor to her, though it made no difference to him. In spite of all this, it did rain. This was a miserable start for the day. It meant that Jane's hair which had been done up in curlers during the night turned into long damp strings.

She arrived at Moose Hall in a very low frame of mind. Better pigtails than these slinky things, she reflected bitterly as she examined herself critically in the dressing-room mirror.

Sylvie tried to comfort her. "I'll brush them around my

finger just before you go in." But they both knew it was really a hopeless undertaking.

Sylvie helped Jane into her costume. It was a white cheesecloth dress with wreaths of large red roses around its neck and waist. While she was dressing, Letitia arrived with her hair still in curlers.

"Imagine comin' through the streets with wiggles in your hair!" marveled Jane.

Letitia put on her white cheesecloth dress. Then she sat down before the mirror and Jane watched her unwind the curlers with expert fingers. The curls came out in long yellow pipes. Jane wondered if Letitia felt jumpy inside, the way she did when she thought about "To a Wild Rose."

As if in answer to her thoughts, Letitia announced calmly, "I may be sick."

"Now?" asked Jane, aghast.

"Might. Any time."

"Even when we're doin' the grand parade?"

"Might."

"Even when we're doin' 'To a Wild Rose'?"

"Might."

Jane swallowed hard and wound one of her straggling

locks around her fingers in pensive silence. Letitia added nothing to this thunderbolt, merely sniffing now and again, touching her nose delicately with her scented pocket handkerchief.

At this moment Miss Chichester rushed in. In a very flurried manner she said, "Ready now for the grand parade."

Jane swiftly glanced at Letitia, in a sudden panic lest she should have to do "To a Wild Rose" all by herself. But Letitia looked calm and resigned.

Sylvie ran the hairbrush hastily and belligerently over Jane's hair for the last time. She set the wreath of large red roses on top of Jane's head. "There," she said. "You look lovely. Where's your partner? Hurry for the grand parade." Sylvie wasn't dancing this afternoon. Her class of older pupils was performing in the evening. "A very elegant affair," said Jane loftily to Letitia, as they joined the procession that marched around the hall.

There was Joe by the piano looking carefree and happy. He had seated the audience and so far as he knew he had made no serious mistakes. To be sure, when Mrs. Mulligan, the wife of the Chief of Police, arrived with her little dog, Sugar, he had placed them in the front row with the im-

portant guests. Miss Chichester had not liked this arrangement at all. "Supposing that Sugar causes a commotion! Mrs. Mulligan should be sitting near the door. Well, it's too late now. Let her stay where she is."

Joe was thinking if he did as well turning pages as he had ushering, that ten cents was clinched. So there he was now turning the pages of Miss Nippon's music as she pounded out the Grand Parade March with verve and vigor. That is, he was turning every time Miss Nippon remembered to say "Turn." She wasn't used to having a turner and often tried to flip the pages over, herself.

"We'd oughter had a rehearsal," thought Joe gloomily. "But maybe she'll get used t' havin' me here after a while."

He certainly hoped she wouldn't endanger his ten cents with her forgetfulness. He considered confiding in Miss Nippon, telling her he had much at stake. However, all thought of that ten cents suddenly vanished! All in a second things changed! From a happy, carefree boy, Joe became in a moment the most morose and melancholy of creatures.

It happened while Jane and Letitia were marching past him. He was making a face at them. Jane was hissing something to him that sounded like, "She may be sick." But what she was talking about or who might be sick he neither knew nor cared. He himself felt sick in another second. For

Miss Chichester had appeared very suddenly and said without so much as a word of warning:

"Joe, you'll have to do the sailor's hornpipe after all. That Chet Pudge has never shown up."

Well, after this Joe hardly ever heard Miss Nippon say "Turn." Sometimes he did and hastily flipped the pages over. But most of the time he was too miserable to hear anything. He couldn't do that sailor's hornpipe. Miss Chichester herself admitted that, after giving him three hours' private instruction one day. Had she forgotten?

Miss Nippon now was getting very annoyed with Joe. She would hiss "Turn," but her turner was just standing by with glazed eyes. This made her music terribly jerky, as she paused on the bottom of each page and waited for him to turn. Things could not go on in this way. She became so agitated her eyeglasses fell off. Sometimes they both grabbed for the page and fumbled dreadfully, or else neither one of them thought to turn it, Miss Nippon counting on Joe and Joe thinking gloomily of the sailor's hornpipe.

He tried to recall some of the steps. How did the old thing go? It was weeks since he had given it a thought. Now all he could remember of it was that you slapped your thighs and stamped your feet. And all the while Miss Nippon was getting more and more fidgety. At the end of this number, she hissed in a voice calculated to fetch anyone up short, "You pay attention, young man. You're boggling the music."

The next dance on the program was "To a Wild Rose."

As Jane and Letitia passed Joe to take their place in the center of the floor, Jane hissed again to Joe, "She said she might
be sick, but she hasn't been yet." This temporarily distracted Joe's mind from the sailor's hornpipe. He watched
Jane, and Letitia in particular, with expectant curiosity.
Miss Chichester came over and stood by the piano. From
time to time she made remarks under her breath about the
dancers.

"Adequate," she murmured. "Hardly a finished performance, however. There! I knew that Jane would forget to
make that turn. Now Letitia's off on the wrong foot. End
it quickly, Miss Nippon, and start the clapping."

The two wild roses bowed and rushed more thankfully
than gracefully from the floor.

Then Miss Chichester said, "Now it's your turn, Joe."
She turned to address the audience.

"Ladies and gentlemen, in the absence of Chester Pudge
who, as you see from the programs, was to perform the
sailor's hornpipe in his own inimitable fashion (his grandfather was a sea captain, so he comes by it naturally), in
the absence then of Chester Pudge, Master Joseph Moffat
has very kindly offered to do this dance. Ladies and gentle-

men, it is with great pleasure that I give you Joseph Moffat in the sailor's hornpipe."

Joe gulped in his breath and said to himself, "Wait 'til I get that Chet Pudge." He stumbled over his heavy boot-strings and wished his corduroy trousers did not squeak so as he marched to the middle of the hall. How he hated to leave that nice, safe place by the piano!

"Mercy on us!" he heard Miss Chichester gasp as he stalked past her; "I didn't know he had those heavy boots on. I thought of course he'd be wearing his dancing shoes."

One pair of shoes was as good as another to Joe when it came to sailor's hornpipes. But he was furious with himself! To think the shoes he had on might have served as a good excuse for not doing the dance. And he hadn't thought of it. Too late now, however. On with the sailor's hornpipe!

Miss Nippon started the lively tune and Joe started to shuffle his feet. He could see it was going to be far worse than he had expected even. Stamp! Stamp! Stamp! Slap! Slap! That's all he could remember of it. A great deal of stamping and slapping. His boots made a terrific clatter and his trousers kept up that whistling and squeaking. He had never felt more foolish and miserable in his whole life. He could hardly hear the music. Miss Chichester kept time by clapping her hands very hard and nodding her head back and forth so that the hairpins flew. Miss Nippon got along beautifully without a turner and just pounded the music out. They all seemed to think the more noise they made the better he could dance.

Stamp! Stamp! Slap! Slap! He kicked his legs and slapped his thighs. What next, he wondered? Was this going on forever?

But what was this? Sugar, Mrs. Mulligan's Sugar, who had slept peacefully in her lap through such dances as "A Daisy-do," "To a Wild Rose," and "Nelly-take-a-kiss," suddenly sat bolt upright. Every nerve in his taut little body was alive and vibrant. He uttered a joyful yelp and bounded from Mrs. Mulligan's lap to the center of the floor where Joe was performing. He stood up on his hind legs, bowed, stamped, shuffled and turned this way and that. Anyone could see he was dancing as perfect a sailor's hornpipe as a small, furry dog possibly could.

"Hurray! Hurray!" shouted the audience as soon as it had recovered from its first bewildered surprise.

Joe was so startled by the new development that he

paused, hoping this was to be deliverance from this miserable dance. Then he realized that the dog, Sugar, was doing the sailor's hornpipe and was looking to him for cues. "Gee, what a smart dog," thought Joe enthusiastically, and took up the steps again. Bow and kick! Shuffle and stamp! The two got on together with perfect understanding.

"Bravo! Bravo!"

"Hurray for Joseph Moffat and hurray for Sugar!"

Storms of applause rocked the hall.

"Again! Again!" the people yelled. "Encore!"

The enthusiasm was so great that Joe and the dog just had to repeat the dance. Joe didn't mind it a bit the second time. "The people are probably lookin' at him, not at me," he thought, almost enjoying himself now.

Finally the music ceased. Sugar gracefully bowed his head several times and then he returned to Mrs. Mulligan, walking all the way on his hind feet. Joe bowed too and retreated hastily to his place by the piano amidst rousing shouts of applause.

"Hurray! Hurray! for Joey Moffat and the dog. Hurray for the sailor's hornpipe!" the audience screamed again.

Joe scrunched his program up in his pocket and wished they'd all stop yelling and clapping. He certainly wished he could get behind the piano, but of course that was impossible with everyone staring so. Besides, there were still one or two dances on the program and he supposed he'd have to resume his job as turner if he wanted that ten cents.

As for Sugar, he climbed right back on Mrs. Mulligan's lap. He was panting and his tongue hung out of his mouth. Mrs. Mulligan petted him and said, "Good doggie! Smart doggie! Where did you learn those tricks, sir?" For no one

in the audience, not even Mrs. Mulligan, knew what had prompted that dance—no one knew that years before he had become Mrs. Mulligan's lap dog he had belonged to a young sailor, a friend of the Chief of Police. This sailor had taught Sugar (not Sugar then, but Tar!) to dance the sailor's hornpipe, while he too danced and played the harmonica.

Well, Sugar hadn't heard that tune in years, and this afternoon when he did hear it, what was he thinking of? A hall filled with party-dressed ladies and children clad in fancy costumes? Not at all; but a rolling deck, a young sailor named Jack, and the taste of salt in the air. Was that why he was licking his whiskers when he settled down once more in Mrs. Mulligan's lap?

When all the dances were finished, Miss Nippon struck up the Grand Parade March again and everyone filed out. Joe waited at the piano, turning until the last chord was played. Then he helped Miss Chichester close up the hall. As they parted she said, "Thank you, Joe, for your impromptu performance. You made a success of the recital. Everyone says you were the best on the program. You certainly were the hit of the day." And she gave him a friendly nod as she put up her umbrella. But she forgot his ten cents and Joe was too shy to ask her for it. He pulled down his cap, jerked up his coat collar, stuck his hands in his pockets, and walked home in the rain, whistling.

7

ANOTHER SIGN ON THE YELLOW HOUSE

JANE WAS POLISHING THE THREE LAMP CHIMNEYS—THE big one for the sitting-room lamp, the medium one for the kitchen, and the little one for the window looking over the porch. She had the little one in her hand. Puff! She blew into it. Her warm breath would loosen the smoke and make it easy to shine clean. First she blew into it: Huff! the small beaded top end. Then she blew into it: Puff! the larger bottom end. The little chimney was the hardest to clean. Her hand just barely fitted into it. Mama couldn't do this one at all. Her hands were too large. When Mama finished with this chimney, there was usually a ring of black around the middle of it that she just couldn't reach from top or bottom. In the end Jane always had to finish this.

As she worked, she stopped occasionally to wipe the tears from her eyes. They just would keep coming. When she finished with the chimneys, she set them in a row on the red checked tablecloth. Then she placed the three lamps on a newspaper on the floor and filled them with kerosene oil. She liked the gurgling noise the oil made as it poured through the funnel to the thirsty lamp. Next she trimmed the wicks neatly and lighted them with fingers that trembled.

This was the first time she had ever been allowed to light the lamps and she felt a little scared. When she had lighted the wicks, she turned them down so the flame was an even line and wouldn't send black smoke up into her clean chimneys. Now very carefully she put the chimneys on and the lamps were ready.

She dabbed the tears away again and went to the window to look out. The windowpane was thickly frosted with beautiful ferns and leaves. Jane blew on it and her warm breath made a clear space for her to peer through. Maybe Joe would be coming. The coal supply had run out and Joe had been sent to the coal yards to fetch a bushel bag on his sled.

Or maybe Sylvie would be running up the street with Edie Ellenbach, coming from choir rehearsal. Or best of all, perhaps Mama herself would be coming with Dr. Belknap, good jolly Dr. Belknap. Because Rufus was ill and Mama didn't know what was the matter with him at all. She had tried all the usual home remedies—mustard plaster, camomile tea, even castor oil. The mere fact that Rufus took all these things without a murmur showed there must be something very wrong with him.

"Oh, please someone come home," said Jane, dashing the tears away. She had to keep rubbing at her clear spot on the windowpane because her breath kept steaming it up. The street lamp-lighter came along, stamping his feet and thrashing his arms about, it was so cold. He had ear-muffs on and his breath came out in great gusts of steam. He lighted match after match and fastened them in his long pole. This he raised carefully to the pilot of the street lamp but the wind kept blowing the matches out. Finally he had to shinny up the post and light it with his hand. Then he closed the little door on the lamp, jumped down, and disappeared up the street, lowering his head against the cold.

When he had gone, Jane felt more lonely and sad than ever. Seeing him light his matches had made her think of "The Little Match Girl." Great tears welled in her eyes, some for Rufus, some for the cold lamp-lighter, some for herself who was no longer Janey Moffat but a poor little match girl, huddling in some doorway and lighting the last match with her poor frozen fingers. . . .

The sound of an automobile sputtering in the cold clear night up New Dollar Street aroused her to action. Maybe this was Dr. Belknap and Mama now! Carefully she took the smallest lamp and placed it in the window over the porch where it would shine a welcome. Then she lighted the feeble gas jet that sent out a pale flickering flame on the wall in the sitting-room. Now all was ready. Feeling excited over all this unaccustomed responsibility, she tiptoed back to the kitchen and started to peel the onions for supper.

The car stopped in front of the yellow house with more loud bangs. It surely must be Dr. Belknap's Ford. It was! She heard Mama's low urgent voice on the porch and the doctor's loud, cheerful one in answer. Jane's heart beat very fast. A visit from the doctor was such a rare event. Usually Mama's remedies were completely successful.

Mama opened the door and in they came, letting in lots of cold crisp air which made the lights in the gas jet and the oil lamps flutter wildly. Mama and the doctor waved their greetings to Janey and disappeared immediately into the front parlor which Mama had made into a bed-room for Rufus. This would separate him from the rest of the family in case what he had was catching.

Janey stood in the kitchen doorway straining her ears, trying to hear what the doctor was saying. Joey and Sylvie arrived together at the back door and tiptoed to her side. Even the usually gay Sylvie looked worried. What was the matter with their Rufus? At last Mama and the doctor came out of Rufus' room. Janey, Sylvie, and Joe caught the last of what he was saying.

". . . a very mild case. Don't worry. Do as I tell you and he will be all right. Good night. Good night, everyone. I'll be back tomorrow. As I leave I'll tack the scarlet fever quarantine sign on the house."

Scarlet fever! A firecracker would not have caused more amazement. Sylvie, Joe, and Janey looked at Mama in consternation. They had seen this sort of sign on other people's houses but never dreamed there would ever be one on theirs. Why, Jane remembered when Edie Ellenbach had scarlet fever, how she would go around the block rather than pass the Ellenbach home. Or if she just had to go that way, she'd hold her nose tightly until she thought she was out of the germ area. She certainly couldn't keep her fingers on her nose for all the time Rufus would be sick. She couldn't help laughing at this foolish idea.

But how many signs were they going to have on the yellow house anyway? There was already the For Sale sign. Now there was going to be Scarlet Fever too! Janey didn't remember ever seeing two signs at the same time on anybody else's house on New Dollar Street. As awful as For Sale and Scarlet Fever were, Janey considered that perhaps there was a certain amount of importance in living in a house that had not one sign but two signs on it.

Now the door closed. The doctor was gone.

There was a deep silence in the yellow house while the tap-tapping of the doctor's hammer rang out in the frosty air. There it was! Scarlet Fever! None of the Moffats said a word. The silence continued until the spluttering of the doctor's car faded away completely down New Dollar Street.

Then Mama broke the silence with a little laugh. "Well, anyway," she said, "at least we will not have to worry about moving for a while. No one will think of buying the yellow house while there is a scarlet fever sign on the door."

Well, there was a little consolation in that thought, but it didn't ease the worry in all their hearts about Rufus. And Jane couldn't help those tears gathering on her lashes again.

The next few weeks were certainly topsy-turvy ones for the Moffats in the yellow house. Rufus was more ill than had first been thought and there was one night when Mama did not go to bed at all. Dr. Belknap came every day up through that night when Rufus was so very sick. The doctor spent most of that night right there in the yellow house. Then he said, "Now he'll begin to get better," and sure enough, Rufus did.

All the while that Rufus was sick, Mama never came into the kitchen and she almost always wore a white mask over her mouth and nose. Joe filled her coal-scuttle several times a day and left it in the kitchen doorway for her.

Sylvie was general manager in the kitchen. She planned the meals. She saw to it that the flatirons were heated each night for the beds upstairs because the bitter cold continued. You could never even see out of the windows. She sang a great deal as she worked and she invented fine tales to tell to Joe and to Jane. On the whole these three Moffats had a very hilarious time keeping house for themselves.

Jane helped a great deal with the cooking. She liked to cook, which Sylvie did not. And sometimes Jane did the sweeping. Sylvie would say to her, "Janey, you'll have to do the sweeping today. I won't have time. There is so much else to do."

It was funny, but this usually happened when Jane was lost in a book. Goodness, but it was hard to put down Andersen's fairy tales and take up the carpet sweeper. So she devised a method of holding the book in one hand and the carpet sweeper in the other. The carpet sweeper she ran up and down, up and down, over and over on the same spot. At the bottom of each page she moved to another spot and there ran the sweeper back and forth, back and forth . . . but sometimes she would forget to move, she would be so lost in "The Snow Queen" or "The Steadfast Tin Soldier," and there she would stand, rooted to the same spot for pages, or until she heard Sylvie coming. Then quickly she would fall to work again and work twice as hard to make up for these lapses.

As for Joe, he had finished the whistle he was making for Rufus and had started making one for himself. He kept the kitchen fire going, the ashes sifted, and the water pipes from freezing. He tried to become more intimate with Catherine-the-cat, but her cold, aloof nature was not to be changed. Mama was the only person she had any use for. And she missed her dreadfully. She tried constantly to break away from this intolerable bondage in the kitchen and get into the sitting-room where Mama was. Finally

she learned there was no use in this. One
of those children foiled her each time. So
she maintained a sullen silence for the rest
of Rufus' illness. Once when Joe tried to
pet her, she jumped up and ran under
the stove with disdainful hisses. This was
very strange considering how gentle Joe
always was and always had been with
animals. "So why," wondered Jane in
exasperation, watching Catherine's two
yellow eyes gleaming in the darkness

under the stove, "why can't you be real friends with Joe?"

The days passed very slowly. Sylvie, Joe, and Jane could
hardly remember the time when Rufus did not have scarlet
fever. Every day the grocery boy came to the back door and
knocked for the grocery order. Joe would call it out to him
through a crack in the door, a half-peck potatoes, a soup
bone, a pound of lentils, or whatever Sylvie needed for the
day, because of course they couldn't even pass a paper list to
the boy lest a germ escape. Later in the day the grocery
boy would come back, leave the supplies on the back stoop,
knock, and run, not taking a good deep breath until he had

gotten way past the empty lot next door.

But now Rufus was beginning to recuperate. He could sit up in bed and he wanted to know every five minutes why he couldn't go out now. Mama had a hard time keeping him amused. She told him stories. She told him the kind that always begins, "Once upon a time . . ." and she told him the kind about when she was a little girl in New York, that always began, "Well, then . . ." or just, "Well . . ."

"Tell about when you were little in New York, Mama," Rufus said.

"Well . . . in New York City where I lived with mother and Tina, my big sister (that's your Tonty) and Nora, my lame sister, when the hurdy-gurdy man came around with his organ and his monkey, the children all danced in the street. That's what they did in the Village anyway, in Greenwich Village where I was born and lived until Sylvie came. Well, Tina and I used to dance too, of course. And Nora would sit up there in the window, so pale and pretty, and clap her hands and watch. All the children in the block came and danced and sang and clapped their hands. And finally when it was all over, the monkey went around collecting pennies in his little red hat. Why,

he used to climb right up to Nora's window on the second floor and take her penny right out of her hand."

And Mama would pause, remembering.

"Took pennies right out of her hand?" Rufus reminded her impatiently.

"Indeed he did. Right out of her hand. She loved it." And again Mama fell silent in her memories until Rufus urged, "Go on, Mama."

"Well, one day when the organ-grinder and his monkey came along, Nora wasn't sitting up there in her usual place by the window. And do you know that monkey missed her! He climbed right up to the second floor and right into our house. When he didn't find her in the front room, he kept looking until he did find her in bed in the back room. He sat on the edge of the bed and made funny faces at Nora. Then he hung by his tail from the gas jet for the longest time. She just screamed with laughter and clapped her hands. The more she laughed the more fancy tricks he did.

"Then, mind you, he paraded around the room bowing and nodding and finally fetched up short right on her bed. He took off his hat then for his usual reward. Well, of course, Nora didn't have any pennies near her and she couldn't get up to get one. So she took a white rose from the vase beside her, broke off the thorns, and gave it to him.

"Oh, he did look comical as he backed out of her room, bowing and scraping with the white rose in his mouth (she told us all about it afterwards). And all the children cheered when he poked his head out of the window, proud as a peacock with that rose. Yes, he sat up there for the longest time, smelling his rose and smelling his rose. The more the children laughed and screamed, the more he smelled his rose. At last he put it in his mouth and climbed down and off they went, the hurdy-gurdy man playing as he left and the monkey sitting on the organ with the rose in his mouth and waving his hat at us all. Oh, he was a comical one," laughed Mama, wiping her eyes with a corner of her blue checked apron.

Tale after tale she told him of when she was little in New York. The magic names she knew! Lillie Langtry! Ada Rehan, the sweetest of them all, acting down at the Booth! Adelina Patti at the Metropolitan Opera House! "Of course we had to sit way up, way up . . . it's bigger than anything you can imagine. But we had opera glasses and could see the elegant people in the boxes in their furs and jewels. I used to go with my cousin Julius. He was a great tease and called himself Julius Hausenchausen-pschutzler . . ." Here, roars of delight from Rufus who never could hear that name without nearly splitting himself in the middle with laughter.

There was no end to her stories.

"Tell about when you learned to ride a bicycle, Mama," Rufus said.

"Oh, that time," laughed Mama, shaking down the pot-bellied stove with a firm hand.

"Tell me, tell me," called Rufus.

"Well then," said Mama, "I'd saved my money and saved my money. What shall I buy, I wondered? I'll buy a bicycle, I thought. So I did. It was very handsome, a bright blue to match my eyes. And I bought a sailor suit, a little deeper blue, to wear when I went bicycling. Oh, it was very handsome, with white braid and all. Well, those bicycles in those days were very different from Joe's. We had a big wheel in front and a tiny one behind."

"Could they go faster?" asked Rufus.

"Well, they could go fast enough as you shall hear. Some bicycles were made for two. You know that song,

'On a bicycle built for two . . .'

But mine wasn't. It was a singleton, just for me. So I practiced on it around Washington Square. Then after a few days I said to myself, 'I'm good enough for Fifth Avenue now.' So I rode onto Fifth Avenue and got going fine. Indeed I got going too fine because as I was sailing past a traffic policeman, he yelled at me:

" 'Hey, stop! You're speeding.'

" 'I can't,' said I. 'I'm just learning.' And by that time I was a block away and I couldn't stop until I'd reached the old Brevoort House. Then I walked my bike back to the policeman. I didn't want to make him angry since I wanted to ride on Fifth Avenue every day."

"Did he arrest you?" asked Rufus eagerly.

"No. He just said to take it easy and he complained about the traffic problem all us bicyclists caused. I wonder what he thinks of all these new-fangled automobiles? Ah, they'll never be as handsome as the horses and broughams, I tell you," she said, smoothing out his pillows.

Leon Slobodkin

"Now can I get up?" demanded Rufus.

"No. Not today. But soon. And see! I'm going to move your bed to a different position. Then you can watch the others in the kitchen and besides, you'll get a better view out of this window onto the porch. The frost is beginning to thaw a little and soon you'll be able to see out altogether. There! How's that now?" she asked, puffing a little from the exertion.

"All right, but I wish I could get up," said Rufus.

8

THE COAL BARGE

JANE WAS SITTING WITH HER FEET IN THE OVEN, WARMING them. She had gotten them wet building a snow man with Rufus. It was good to have Rufus to play with again. For now Rufus was all over the scarlet fever. He was back at school. They were all back at school. Several colonies had been settled in Janey's absence. Hard words like squirrel and school had been taken up in Rufus' class; and Washington had crossed the Delaware in Joe's. Sylvie was back at choir rehearsals. And now the children could go anywhere they liked in the whole block, in the whole town in fact. Most important of all the Scarlet Fever sign was off the door. If only they had taken that old For Sale sign down too, thought Jane.

"Mama, do you think, now that we're not contagious any more, that someone will come and buy our house?"

"Someone might, but let's hope not until the cold weather is over anyway," replied Mama.

"Well, why couldn't we have left the Scarlet Fever sign on the door so no one would want to buy this house?" asked Jane.

"You couldn't have gone to school then. Not as long as the Scarlet Fever sign was on the door. Would you like that?"

"No-o-o, I s'pose not," answered Jane thoughtfully. She felt her toes. They seemed to be quite dry, so she went into the Grape Room to cut out a cardboard sole to fit in her shoes which had worn a hole right through to the ground. The Moffats were feeling the pinch of hard times this winter. The quarter meter ate up the quarters for gas so quickly —and coal! "A lump of coal is as valuable as a gold nugget," Mama said. Joe had to sift the ashes and resift them for possible good coals.

"Are we poverty stricken, Mama?" Jane asked, returning to the kitchen with her new sole comfortably in place.

"No, Janey. Not poverty stricken," said Mama soberly, and stroking Janey's cheek, "not poverty stricken, just . . ."

"Rich, then?" asked Jane.

"No. Not rich either, nor well-to-do, just poor . . ." answered Mama.

This satisfied Jane, for she thought if they were poverty stricken she would have to go out into the cold and into the streets and sell matches like the little match girl. But she knew from the way the silver coins left Mama's hands when she was paying for the potatoes that fingers and coins parted company reluctantly. And the truth is Mama was having to be a very careful manager to make ends meet. She had not been able to do any sewing while Rufus had scarlet fever. Moreover the ladies in the town of Cranbury decided they would have to do without new dresses since times were so bad. They said, "Why have a gown made by hand when you can really pick them up so inexpensively in the shops nowadays?" There were many days when Mama and Madame had no sewing to do at all. Miss Chichester was the only steady customer and that was because there was that arrangement about the dancing lessons.

But finally, thank goodness, someone had decided that the little boys in town should organize into a Naval Reserve Corps. Joe was in it and Mama was to make all the white sailor suits. This was a job! Fifty of them! For days and weeks Madame had looked altogether ridiculous with white middy blouses on her shoulders.

"Here," said Mama to Joe when he came in from school that afternoon. "Take this five dollar bill and buy a bushel of coal. Count the change very carefully. That's the last bill we'll have until these sailor suits are ready."

Jane said she would go with Joe. Rufus wanted to go too but Mama said he couldn't. He had played outdoors enough for one day, as he didn't have all his strength back yet after his illness.

Joe dragged Jane over the hard icy pavement on his Flexible Flier sled. She sat on the empty burlap bag that was to hold the coal. The short winter day was already breathlessly hurrying to an end. A strong wind had arisen and the going was difficult. The lamp-lighter was already making his rounds. Otherwise, very few people were on the street this cold day and they were muffled up like mummies. They passed Peter Frost. He was belly-flopping on his Flexible Flier.

"Hello, Moffats," he said sneeringly, pretending he was going to bump smack into them but veering quickly aside just before crashing. His tone had improved very little since the ghost in the attic, but at least he no longer pulled Sylvie's curls and Jane's braids. He didn't honk his bicycle siren right in their ears, nor did he bark like a dog at Catherine-the-cat. On the whole, he treated all the Moffats with just a shade more respect.

Joe and Jane did not answer but trudged on. The wind made their scarves flutter madly and tried to snatch their hats from their heads. It put bright red spots on the ends of their noses but it couldn't get at their ears, for Joe's fur-lined muffs prevented that as did Jane's hand-crocheted red woolen tam.

"Be easier comin' back," shouted Joe, his breath coming out in white puffs.

They stopped for a few minutes in the shelter of a fruit and grocery store. The lights from the window shone on the ice and snow. Jane and Joey pressed their faces against the window and looked hungrily at the oranges, apples, tangerines, and grapefruit.

"Oh, my mouth's waterin' so," said Jane. "I can't see a window full of oranges without my mouth just waterin' and waterin'."

"Me—apples," put in Joe, thinking of the crunch of putting his teeth into one of them.

"Oh, come on, come on," said Jane, dancing up and down, for her chilblains hurt her. "I can't abide to look at those oranges any longer."

So on they went. Way at the end of the street, on the harbor's edge, they could see the big sign C O A L. The

letters were so high you could see them a mile away. The nearer they came to the water, the keener the wind howled. They talked little, keeping their noses buried in their mufflers. At last they reached the coal yards. Here there was a little protection from the wind, but goodness, how cold it was! The cold crept inside their mackintoshes and made their bodies shrink into tight little balls.

A big man with icicles in his mustache and a face blackened with coal-dust asked them what they wanted.

"A bushel of coal, please," said Joe, handing the man the burlap bag.

The big man led the way to the coal sheds where each different kind of black coal had its own stall. The coal man filled the bag with the shining black nuggets.

"Boy, oh, boy," whispered Jane, "don't you wish't all that coal was in our own barn?"

"All right," said the man, lugging the bag to the sled. "A dollar and twenty cents."

Joe felt in his pocket for the money. It wasn't there! His heart leaped into his throat. Hadn't he put that five dollar bill in his coat pocket? The little pocket with the flap that buttoned? He felt again very carefully. There was no hole in it. But the money certainly was not there. His hands trembled as he began hastily to feel in all the other pockets.

Jane looked at him in helpless horror. The man stood there like a rock and said nothing. Joe gulped. In all his pockets, nothing! Could he have lost it? Lost all the money they had?

"Maybe you took the money," he said to Jane, knowing very well this wasn't the case, but hoping anyway.

Jane shook her head but she felt in her pockets. Oh, if only her fingers would close on that worn, little black purse! But no, nothing!

The two stood there in front of the coal man in the utmost dejection. Between the gusts of wind they could hear the ice making in the harbor. Joe went through his pockets again. Perhaps he had missed it? No. There was nothing that his fingers could possibly mistake for money.

They were so dismayed they could say nothing. Silently the coal man took the burlap bag off the sled, dragged it across the yard with a grunt, dumped the coal back into its shed, handed the empty burlap bag back to Joe, took out a quid of tobacco and said:

"No money, no coal."

Jane and Joe trudged out of the coal yards. The empty sled spun around crazily on the ice behind them. Jane didn't even feel like being pulled on the sled. It was hard not to cry.

"Shucks!" said Joe. "We'll find it. We'll retrace our steps exactly. We'll go slow and look on both sides of the path."

But the wind was now on their backs and urged them up the street swiftly. It laid giant palms on their backs and tried to hurry them along. The empty sled kept knocking

into Joe's heels. They
fought the wind every
inch of the way, trying to
go slowly to look for the
purse.

Once Jane thought she
saw it. "There it is," she
screamed, pointing to
something black
under a street
lamp. But it was only a small black mitten some child had
lost.

Joe was looking on the right side. Jane was looking on
the left. They didn't miss one inch of the way. They didn't
see the oranges in the grocery store window this time nor
did they notice Mr. Pudge driving by in a real sleigh, a
real sleigh on runners. Why, you hardly ever saw a real
sleigh any more, but Jane and Joe didn't notice it.

Twilight deepened. The bright yellow trolleys were
crowded with men coming home from their work in New
Haven. Mr. Shoemaker, Mr. Ellenbach, and Mr. Horn
all got off at New Dollar Street and walked up the street

talking and joking together. They turned their collars up and thrashed their arms about to keep warm. It was good to have company, to smell Mr. Ellenbach's cigar, to hear Mr. Shoemaker's hearty laugh, thought Jane.

But the darker it grew, the more false alarms they had about the lost purse. Every shadow from every piece of ice or snow was pounced upon, but with diminishing fervor. And here they were turning into the gate of the yellow house with no coal and no money.

The little kerosene lamp shone through the feathery ferns of the frosted windowpane. They wiped their feet on the doormat and entered. They stood disconsolately for some seconds, blinking their eyes and blowing their noses. They listened to the sounds coming from other parts of the house that indicated what the rest of the family was doing. Mama was in the Grape Room, running the sewing machine like sixty to finish some of those middy blouses. Sylvie was preparing the supper in the kitchen and singing a song Mama had been teaching her, a French song called "Au Clair de la Lune." She would sing some of the lines and then call out to Mama, "Was that right, Mama?"

And Mama would stop the sewing machine long enough

to sing out the right words and tune.

Every time Mama stopped the whirring of the sewing machine, they could hear a rattling noise that indicated

Rufus was playing with his marbles on the uncarpeted floor of the Grape Room.

Joe and Jane stood warming their hands by the pot-bellied stove in the sitting-room, feeling very much out of the family scene. How could they tell Mama about the five dollars being gone? It would be easier almost to go back out of the house and never come back. That's what they thought. "The last we'll have," she had said, "until these sailor suits are finished." Goodness only knew when that might be! No coal until then, did that mean? Joe looked at the coal-scuttle. Just half full. It wouldn't even last through the night.

Sylvie had heard them come in. She danced into the sitting-room, still singing. Now she sang, "Oh, where is the coal?" to the tune of "Au Clair de la Lune . . ."

Jane said, "We lost the money."

"Lost the money!" repeated Sylvie, aghast.

"Yes, I lost the money," said Joe.

Rufus came into the sitting-room on all fours in pursuit of an aggie that had gotten out of his hands and gone careening from corner to corner.

"Lost the money!" repeated Rufus, forgetting the runaway marble.

The four stood around the stove in consternation. How could they tell Mama? Their last five dollars!

The whirring of the sewing machine stopped and stayed stopped. Mama went into the kitchen to see how Sylvie was getting along with the dinner. Not finding her there, she entered the sitting-room.

"Goodness! What long faces! Whatever is the matter?"

"I lost the money," said Joe.

"Lost the money?" said Mama.

For a few seconds there was silence. A hot coal fell from the grate and rolled to the carpet where Mama swiftly scooped it up with the coal shovel before it had a chance to burn a hole. Joe knew he had never felt as miserable as this before in his whole life. It was certainly a far worse feeling than the time he had had to do the sailor's hornpipe, and nearly as bad as the night Rufus was so ill. This thing was his fault entirely. What could he do to make up for it? He prayed for a tremendous snowstorm. He might earn it back by shoveling sidewalks. But there wasn't likely to be snow with the weather this cold. The other Moffats, knowing how miserable he was feeling as he stood there with his hands stretched to the stove and his face as expressionless as that doorknob there, felt scarcely less miserable.

Mama finally said, "Well, if it's gone, it's gone. We'll manage somehow. If I work late tonight, I might finish some of the suits by tomorrow."

This was horrible, thought Joe. Mama work late because he had lost the money! He just couldn't help having a huge lump in his throat. He blinked his eyes hard and fixed them with a stare on the mantel. Of course he wasn't going to make matters worse by crying in front of them all. As he stared up there, he gradually became aware of a small black purse on the clock. Why . . . why . . . why, there it was!

"Oh," he gasped. The relief was almost too great to bear. "There it is, there it is! I musta laid it on the clock when I was warmin' my mittens by the stove. I remember now. That's what I did."

Joe's spirits climbed to the sky. He took a shin-donnegan over every chair. He grabbed the purse, pulled his cap down over his ears, and ran out of the house. He snatched his Flexible Flier and was halfway up the street before Jane caught up with him.

"You don't have to come again if you don't want," said Joe.

"I do want," said Jane. "Mama said you could wait though, and go in the morning before school if you'd ruther."

"D'ruther go now. Get on," he ordered.

Jane sat on the sled and Joe felt so good he ran like a racehorse, kicking bits of ice and snow into Jane's lap all the way to the end of New Dollar Street. When they

turned the corner, the wind was too strong for this. So Joe
gave the rope to Jane and pushed her instead by the shoulders. She bent over like the letter C and listened to the
hard scrunching of Joe's heels in the hard snow.

"Comin' back'll be easy," he panted.

"Yup," she answered.

When they arrived at the coal yard, it was inky black.
The man with the icicles in his whiskers was locking up the
office. He had a smoky oil lantern in his hands and said,
"Too late for coal tonight. Scoot!"

Scoot? Not Joe. This time he'd get his coal.

"We been here before today," he said.

The man raised the smoky lantern and peered into Joe's
face. Then into Jane's. They held their breath.

"H-m-m. Well, come along." And he led the way across
the coal yard. It was pitch black now and the children kept
close to the man with the lantern. Jane clutched Joe by the
arm. This was a hobgoblin kind of a place, she thought,
looking to the left and right. Suddenly the black was dis-
pelled by the appearance of the moon. The wind had tossed
aside its mantle of clouds for a time and there the moon was,
radiant.

"Look how fast it's goin'," said Jane.

"Yeh," said Joe. "Only it's the clouds that's goin', not the moon."

As the man shoveled the coal into the bag again, the children walked to the edge of the wharf. The harbor looked as though it were frozen tight. But far out they could see a black space where the water still defied the cold.

"Boy, oh, boy, I'd hate to fall into that water," said Joe, shivering as they returned to their sled. The man lugged the bag over to them and with loud grunts placed it on their sled. Joe handed him the five dollar bill. The moon disappeared again. So the man had to count the change out of his dirty black canvas bag by the light of the lantern. Joe bent close too in order to see that the change was right.

When all this was satisfactorily settled, the man said, "Now scoot! I want me supper!"

Joe and Jane dragged the heavy sled across the barren coal yard. They were glad to be going home. They were good and tired and were thankful for the help the wind gave them in pulling the heavy sled. At last, here they were at the yellow house again. They drew the sled around to the back entry. Joe dragged the coal to the box in the corner.

Scraping their feet hard on the mat, they entered the kitchen. Catherine-the-cat gave an angry m-r-r-r at having a draught on her back. They sniffed the potato pancakes that Mama had made fresh for them. Mama's face was rosy from standing over the stove. The others had all eaten and gone into the sitting-room. Joe and Jane sat down. Mama put the plates of steaming pancakes before them.

"Too bad you had to go twice," she said, stroking their cold cheeks.

9

SHARE AND SHARE ALIKE

AT LAST THE TERRIFIC COLD WEATHER HAD GONE. NOW IT was spring. The ground was soft and spongy and the lilacs were in bloom. Jane sat on the hitching post, carefully holding in her moist palm the first few violets she had just found and watching Joe and Rufus. They were over in front of the yellow house practicing on their stilts. Of course Joe was doing very well, but Rufus found that walking on stilts was quite a lot more difficult than just walking on his own two legs. On stilts his legs kept going wider and wider apart all the time so that he had to jump off and begin all over again. Jane couldn't help it; she had to laugh at him. He looked so funny. But Rufus didn't care.

Now and then Joe rested against the front of the yellow house. Once he leaned against the For Sale sign.

"That old sign!" he muttered.

"Why don't you tear it down?" asked Jane, responding to Joe's irritation.

"Can't. But I'll fix it up a bit," said Joe. He took a red chalk from his pocket and changed the S into a $ sign.

Jane looked at his work in silent approval. The For Sale sign was weather-beaten and dingy but it most certainly was still there. Now that the warm weather had arrived, a few prospective buyers had come to examine the house. Mama said she would look for another house for them to live in. She didn't like living in a house that might be sold over her head at any minute. But the children begged her not to move until they really had to. "Maybe no one will buy it," they said. For the sign had been there a long time and no one had bought the yellow house yet.

Jane swung around on the hitching post. Of all the houses on New Dollar Street, theirs was the only one with a For Sale sign on it. Why did it have to be *their* house? Because it was the best one, of course.

Now she watched Mr. Brooney, the grocery man, drive up with his horse and wagon. The Moffats called Mr. Brooney's horse the dancey horse because of the graceful way he threw his legs about when he cantered up the street. Mr. Brooney stopped between Mrs. Squire's house and the yellow house. He threw down the heavy iron weight to keep his horse from dancing away and took several baskets of groceries from the wagon. He crossed the street and disappeared in Mrs. Frost's back yard. He was gone a long time. The horse stood there with the greatest patience. Occasionally he flicked his long tail to rid himself of a pesky fly. Or now and then he wriggled an ear when Sylvie, who was practicing her graduation music, hit a high note. And sometimes he raised one dainty foot or another and then planted it firmly on the ground. For the most part, however, he stood there dreamily, looking neither to left nor to right

Jane watched him and watched him.

He had wings and could carry her away.

He was the wooden horse of Troy and many men could

step out of him.

He was a bridge that she could walk under.

Sitting up there on the hitching post, watching the horse and watching the horse, Jane repeated to herself, "The horse is a bridge for me to walk under, and I'm goin' to walk under it."

So she jumped down and marched over to the horse. He stood there immobile. Except for his eyes which followed her around like those of the velvet-clad lady in the picture in the sitting-room.

Jane walked under him and came out on the other side. This gave her an extraordinary feeling of satisfaction and elation.

At that moment when Jane was walking under the horse, Mama came to the window of the front parlor and shook her duster out vigorously. "Thank heavens!" she said to herself; "thank heavens, it's spring again and that long hard winter is over." No more fussing with stoves and wondering where the next coal was coming from, she thought, slapping the duster against the green shutters. And better still, there was lots of work to do. Tilly Cadwalader was getting married. Mama had not only the bridal outfit to make but the bridesmaids' gowns too. The yellow house was just bulging with white satin and tulle, with billowy yellow and lavender tulle. It was to be a really elegant affair that would keep her busy and the pantry full for some time, she thought with satisfaction.

But goodness! Could Mama believe her eyes? What was Janey doing? Walking under that horse! Of all things! Mama was speechless with amazement and dropped the duster out of the window at the sight. Joe and Rufus saw her from the other side of the yard and became all tangled up in their stilts in consequence. Sylvie, who was practicing her singing way back in the kitchen, was the only one who did not see her.

"Jane! Whatever on earth!" Mama cried. "You mustn't do such things. You mustn't walk under horses. They might kick or start walking or something."

Jane stepped thoughtfully up the walk. "All right, Mama," she said.

She had no desire to keep on walking under horses. It was just something she felt she had to do at that moment, just that once. And she knew that horse. She'd been watching him and watching him. So she had walked under him

and from the feeling inside of her she thought it had turned out to be an all right sort of thing to do—just that once.

Joe and Rufus resumed their stilt-walking. Their sister Jane sometimes did extremely curious things, they agreed.

Mama called to Jane to hand her her duster. Mama was still disturbed about Jane walking under that horse. Of course she was used to unexpected things happening. After all, with four such children that was only natural. But walk-ing under a horse, now! That was different and dangerous. It is true that Jane herself had no further desire or interest in walking under a horse again. But Mama had no way of knowing this. Goodness! For all she knew, Jane might make a habit of this. Best send her on some errand and get her mind off horses.

"Jane," she said, "run down the street to Tilly Cad-walader's and ask her to just slip on this sleeve for the length."

Mama carefully wrapped the sleeve in white tissue paper. She told Jane not to run and to be very careful. If anything happened to that sleeve, she didn't know what she'd do because there wasn't any more satin and goodness only knows . . . "Why, maybe Tilly couldn't get married at all if anything happens to this sleeve, and that would be a dreadful thing, a dreadful thing altogether," said Mama, chuckling.

Jane took the package and walked as carefully up the street as though she were carrying a lemon meringue pie. The Cadwaladers lived in a sleepy-looking gray house across the street from Chief Mulligan's. The shingles protruded over each window like languorous, drooping eyelids. "I bet they close like eyes after everyone has gone to bed," thought Jane, grinning to herself as she rang the bell. There was a good deal of suspense in ringing the Cadwaladers' bell. There were seven Cadwalader sisters. Of course you never knew which one of them would open the door. When the door opened, you had the excitement of thinking fast to say the right Hello: Hello, Tilly, Hello, Milly, Hello, Molly, Polly, Lollie, or Hello, Olly. And last, Hello, Nelly. "Like the game of beast, bird or fish almost," laughed Jane as the door swung open.

This time it was "Hello, Tilly," the eldest and the only Cadwalader girl who wore her hair high on her head.

Jane stepped into the front parlor. She snuffed the air here. This house had a different sort of smell altogether

from the yellow house. She handed the sleeve to Tilly. Tilly
tried it on. The six other sisters stood around saying Oh,
and Ah. Milly Cadwalader wanted to see how Tilly would
look as a bride. She snatched down one of the lace curtains

and held it on Tilly's head. Yes, she was a bride with the
satin sleeve and the lace curtain on. All the sisters clapped
their hands and laughed and one thumped "Here comes the
bride" on the small organ.

Then Milly, Lollie, Polly, Olly and last of all, little
Nelly, had each one to play at being the bride. When this
was done, Tilly carefully folded the sleeve into the tissue
paper again and then she reached for the bank that stood

between a Dresden shepherd and his shepherdess. This bank was made out of an orange.

"How did you ever make it?" marveled Jane politely.

"Just scooped out the insides," said Tilly carelessly. She skillfully coaxed out a nickel for Jane with a nail file.

"There," she said. "Thank you so much for coming way down here with the sleeve. Tell your mother it fits beautifully and looks beautiful. You think she will surely have everything ready on time?"

"Oh, yes," replied Jane. "I'm helpin' with the bastings."

Jane was anxious to be off. The nickel burned in her pocket. As she said good-by to all the Cadwalader girls who waved their handkerchiefs and aprons after her, she was thinking about all the good things a nickel can buy.

She raced home with the sleeve. She handed it to Mama who was sewing now in the Grape Room. Sylvie was working in her small patch of vegetable garden which she had planted just the day before. Joe and Rufus had disappeared somewhere with their stilts. Jane clutched the nickel tightly in her fist and walked slowly up the street. She stopped in the Brick Lot to see if any more violets were up yet. There were three with lovely long stems! She picked these and continued on her way down the street towards the railroad tracks. She was going to Mr. Brooney's store. She would surprise them all with something awfully good.

It was lucky there were four of them, she thought. Everything divided so beautifully into four parts. Sylvie, Joe, Jane, and Rufus could not imagine how it would feel if there were just three of them, or five of them, or any other number of them. Imagine having to divide into three parts like the Pudges. Or seven like the Cadwaladers! "I suppose they are used to it, though," she thought. But this way, having four in the family, everything was so easy. Cut a piece of chocolate into four parts. No difficulty at all. Or there was one apiece of four-for-a-penny caramels; or a half apiece of two-for-a-penny peppermints. Yes, it was very convenient having four in the family. "When we grow up we shall each have four children," said Jane to herself, "so things will always be easy to divide." Share and share alike was the rule of the Moffat household and no one ever thought to dispute it.

And now there was this five cents from Tilly Cadwalader. Think of all the fine things it might buy. Twenty caramels, ten sticks of licorice, one ice-cream cone—but that was foolish. An ice-cream cone cannot be divided. Ten peppermint patties, four sheets of paper dolls, one ice-cream cone. "One ice-cream cone" danced before her eyes. It was a hot day for May. It would be nice to taste your first ice-cream cone on a day like this when you had also found your first violets. Oh, if that five cents would only grow into four five cent pieces!

But here she was at Brooney's. Somehow or other her feet marched her right over to the ice-cream counter. No more hesitating over what that nickel was going to buy. Something inside had decided for her. A small, thin voice—Jane knew it was none of hers—said, "One ice-cream cone, please. Strawberry."

Jane sat on the bread-box, kicking her legs against the sides. The ice-cream cone was absolutely delicious. At least the first few bites were delicious. But the more she ate, the less she enjoyed it. She was a pig, that's what, a pig. She found she couldn't eat the last few bites of the cone at all. She gave it to Mr. Brooney's little yellow dog, Jup, who gobbled it up without the least trace of enthusiasm, as though he were doing her a favor in fact.

She sat there disconsolately for some minutes. The few violets she had picked had wilted in her moist hand. She gave them to little Gretta Brooney who was delighted with them. Jane banged her feet against the bread-box. She thought of the bag of sweets she might have had. She could have surprised them all! How pleased and excited everyone would have been. Instead of that she was nothing but an old pig. She started for home, thoroughly ashamed and angry with herself. None of the others would have done such a thing. Well, she never would again, of that she was sure.

When she reached home, she found that even Catherine-the-cat had been faithful to the share and share alike principle and had brought four new little kittens to the yellow house. Catherine brought four kittens every year, one for each

of the Moffat children. This year she had hidden them
in the barn until they were old enough to hold up their
wobbly heads and stand on their shaky legs. So on this day
she had brought them into the yellow house for Mama to
see.

Mama found an old wooden soap-box for them and there
they were, wagging their heads when Jane came in. Sylvie,
Joe, and Rufus were all sitting on the floor watching them.

"We been waitin' for you," said Rufus, beside himself
with excitement. "We're going to do the choosing now."

Choosing their kitten was a game they played every year.
This was great sport, the only sad thing about it being
the thought that they would have to part with their new
pets as soon as Mama could find homes for them. This was
never difficult, for there wasn't a better mouser in the whole
town of Cranbury than Catherine and it was expected that
her kittens would inherit this skill.

"Oh, aren't they cunning?" gasped Jane as Sylvie lifted
each one of them out of the box.

The kittens would try to stand on their shaking legs. But
this was very hard for them and every few minutes they
would fall into sitting positions. There they would remain

for a time, heads wobbling foolishly from side to side. Then they would try again this exciting business of walking. The four kittens seemed quite bewildered at all the strange people, the strange world. All except one. This one, a ball of gray fuzz, with

 perfectly enormous feet, leaped into the air a few times and then started on a tour of exploration. Every few steps she would fall down. But she kept right on trying. There was no doubt that this kitten was the most enterprising of the four.

Rufus burst out laughing at her. "Gee, I hope I win that one," he said.

That was what they all hoped. The little gray one was the favorite.

"Oh, let this one be mine,"

 Jane prayed, although she felt she didn't deserve any

such luck after spending that whole five cents on herself.

The children looked the kittens over and decided on temporary names for them. The little gray one they called Boots because of her truly extraordinary feet. Another kitten they named Mask. This one was black all over except for its face, which was white. It was Rufus who thought up the name Mask for it. Another they called Whiskers and the last one they named Funny because she had one green eye and one blue eye. Next Sylvie wrote each of these four names on four pieces of paper. These she dropped into Mama's hat.

"Now, who will be the one to draw out the names?" Sylvie asked.

"Rufus! Rufus!" cried Joe and Janey. "Because he is the littlest."

"All right," said Sylvie. "Whichever cat has his name drawn by Rufus will be set in the middle of the room. Then we will all go to the four different corners of the room and call, Kitty, Kitty. Whichever person that kitten goes to, why, that person will be the winner of that kitten."

Sylvie had thought this game up years ago and they all loved it.

So now Rufus closed his eyes, put his chubby fist into the

hat, and drew out the first name. They waited with bated breath while Sylvie read the name.

"Funny!" she said.

A cheer went up as Funny was put in the middle of the room.

"Kitty, kitty, kitty," the children called from the four corners of the room. In this game it was possible that you might have a preference for one or another of the four kittens. But this must never be evident. You must call as fervently for this one as that one.

"Kitty, kitty, kitty," they called to the little one named Funny.

"Mu-u-r-r." A very feeble, wistful cry came from Funny. She turned around with difficulty. She was feeling terribly alone in a strange world. Suddenly she rushed as fast as she could towards Jane. However, walking in a straight line was utterly impossible for her and it was Sylvie's corner she finally ended up in. So Sylvie and Funny were out of the game.

Rufus scrunched up his face, put his hand in the hat again. The name was—Whiskers!

Whiskers! Cheers again. But Whiskers didn't care. He

just sat there with his head nodding on his shoulders. looking as though he were going to fall asleep at any moment.

"Kitty, kitty, kitty," Joe, Jane, and Rufus coaxed.

Whiskers just sat there and looked around the room with a pleasant though simple expression.

"Come, Whiskers. Come, kitty," they pleaded again.

But Whiskers just sat there, swaying gently to and fro.

"We shall have to go nearer to this one," said Joey in the manner of a patient parent.

Joey, Jane, and Rufus drew nearer, to within a few feet of Whiskers. Still he just sat.

"He doesn't want to play," said Rufus in disgust.

Now the three went right up close to him. Just a kitten's length away. At this, Whiskers stood up on his shaky legs and staggered nonchalantly over to Rufus. He nestled comfortably on his sleeve and was asleep in a second. So Rufus and Whiskers were out of the game too.

Now just Boots and Mask were left. And Joe and Jane.

"Oh, please let Boots be mine," Jane prayed again and again. "Although of course I know I don't deserve it," she added.

Rufus drew again. This time the name was—Boots.

Boots! The children all cheered lustily. Boots herself seemed full of excitement. All the while the game had been going on, she had been clawing at the soap box and miaowing madly to get out. Now she was out!

"Oh, be mine, be mine," breathed Jane.

"Look at the big toes on her," Joe marveled. "Boy, oh, boy, I hope I win her."

Of course Joe was just as anxious for Boots as Jane was. And why shouldn't he be? Of these four sweet kittens she alone showed marks of personality that lifted her above the usual run of cats and kittens. She paid no attention to Joe or to Jane. Instead she raced madly around the room. She whacked at a tassel that was hanging from the red plush chair. This caused her to lose her balance and she rolled over and over. Up again. She resumed her swift, though wobbly, adventuring through the sitting-room, the new world.

"Oh, pussy, come. Come, pussy," Jane begged.

Boots ran right over to Jane's corner but then, just as she was within a cat's length of her, she backed off to the middle of the room. What a kitten!

"Come, kitty, come, kitty," said Joey in that gentle voice of his that surely Boots would not be able to resist.

Now Boots teetered over towards Joe. She sat down not far from him and stared at him with her big blue eyes. Her little pink tongue was hanging out and she was thoroughly irresistible. Suddenly she began to purr. She was the first one to purr and she sounded like a little engine.

"She's going to Joey," mourned Jane. "Well, of course I don't deserve her."

But at this moment Boots suddenly turned right about again. She jumped wildly into the air a couple of times and then, in a series of little sidewise leaps, she landed right in Jane's lap. Tears came into Jane's eyes. "She's mine. She's mine," she cried, burying her nose in Boots' sweet-smelling fur.

So Mask went to Joey and he immediately found many engaging things about this kitten that they had not yet discovered. For instance, he had the longest fur, the prettiest markings, the longest tail, and many other unusual qualities. Moreover he was the smallest of the four and would need special attention.

At this moment Catherine-the-cat came in. She looked around the room disdainfully. Then she jumped into the soap-box and whirrupped for her kittens. Janey gave Boots one last hug. She already loved this little kitten so much it was almost more than she could bear. She put the kitten carefully back into the soap-box as the other children were doing with theirs. And the choosing game was over.

Joe and Rufus went back to the yard to continue their stilt walking. Sylvie went into the Grape Room to help Mama with the Tilly Cadwalader wedding dress. Janey went out to the big old lilac bush at the side of the house. What a mixed-up sort of day it had been! This day she had walked under a horse, been a pig about an ice-cream cone, and won Boots, the sweetest of all kittens, though she didn't deserve it.

10

MUD AND MURDOCKS

SOMETIMES JANEY JUST HATED THE SIGHT OF THAT OLD weather-beaten sign—For Sale! More and more people were beginning to inquire about the yellow house. Particularly on Sundays when they were out for a stroll in their best clothes.

"Look!" they would say. "Here's a house that's for sale." Then they would walk in the yard and poke their noses into everything as though the yellow house already belonged to them. This made all the Moffats very angry. But what could they do? For instance, take the Murdocks. Of all those who had come to look at the house so far, the Murdocks were easily the most difficult to endure.

Jane felt somewhat to blame for the Murdocks. They might never have noticed the For Sale sign on the yellow house in the first place if it hadn't been for her.

This is the way it happened. One warm Sunday the Murdocks were out taking a walk. They couldn't have chosen a worse time to be strolling up New Dollar Street because that was the very day when Janey felt she simply could not abide the sight of that For Sale sign any more, and in a burst of temper had picked up great chunks of mud and thrown them with splendid aim right at it. By the time she had finished, you couldn't tell whether that sign said Measles, For Sale, or what! It was a mass of mud stains.

Naturally it didn't stay that way long. Mama came out, scolded Jane, gave her a pail of soapy water and a mop and made her scrub off the mud. It was just at that moment those Murdocks came up New Dollar Street, stopped to see what Jane was doing, exclaimed, "Why, this house is for sale!" and marched right in the front gate.

That had been the first time the Murdocks came. Since then they had a way of appearing at the yellow house at most inopportune moments. One minute there wouldn't be any Murdocks around and everything would be lovely, and the next minute there would be Murdocks all over the place.

They were in and out of the house, all around the yard, tasting a cherry from this cherry tree, examining the currant and the raspberry bushes. They were up on the roof tapping the tin, peering down the chimney. They were in and out of the barns. They were just everywhere, and not just once. Hardly a day in the week went by without all the Murdocks or some of the Murdocks attacking the Mof-

fats with their endless questions.

"We might as well set up beds for them!" Mama grumbled.

Altogether there were only four Murdocks, although they seemed more. There were Mr. and Mrs. Murdock, the father and the mother. Then there were the two children—Milton, who was about Rufus' age, and Letitia—the very same Letitia Murdock who had danced "To a Wild Rose" with Janey at Miss Chichester's dance recital. She wore her hair in corkscrew curls every day—not just Sundays and dancing recital days.

The important question with the Murdocks was: "Shall we buy this house?"

It seemed they just couldn't make up their minds all at once. "Well, Lottie," Mr. Murdock would say, "how about it? The yard is very nice with all these fruit trees and we can put improvements in the house."

Then Mrs. Murdock would shake her head slowly, wrinkle up her face with worry lines, and say, "Well, I don't know about living in a house with only one flight of stairs in it. Moreover, isn't it awfully near the railroad tracks?"

Sometimes it was Mrs. Murdock who was all in a mood

for buying it. Then Mr. Murdock would shake his head and say, "I don't know about that roof. It leaks in some spots. It'll be a costly job to fix it the right way."

This went on for such a time that the Moffats wondered if it would ever end.

One warm day the Moffats climbed to the top of Shingle Hill for a nice picnic. There they had spent the day picking wild flowers and taking turns looking through Joey's new binoculars at East Rock, West Rock, and the Sleeping Giant. By the end of the afternoon they were very tired. Janey and Rufus could hardly drag their feet the last few steps down New Dollar Street. Then when they finally reached the yellow house, what did they see? Those Murdocks sitting on the front porch waiting for them. It was a sight to make anyone cry. This time they said they had come around to see where they could put sockets supposing they decided to buy the house and wanted to install electricity. Mama unlocked the door for them and then the Moffats fell into the cane chairs on the porch to wait until the Murdocks had finished their electrical survey. Tired though they were, the Moffats couldn't help feeling awed at the thought of electricity in the yellow house.

Naturally the Moffats were all getting very annoyed at the sight of those Murdocks. They wished the Murdocks could make up their minds once and for all. Did they want to buy the yellow house or did they not? If they did, all right. They, the Moffats, would move out. If they did not, let the Murdocks please go away and leave them alone.

In exasperation Mama finally put on her gloves and her hat, went down the street, and complained to Dr. Witty.

"Dr. Witty," she said, "please do something about those Murdocks. Life in the yellow house is being ruined by them."

Dr. Witty nodded his head thoughtfully up and down and said he'd do the best he could. But of course, well, after all—he did want to sell the house and if it had to be to Murdocks, it had to be to Murdocks.

For a while things were better. All the Murdocks didn't arrive every other day. But they did keep coming, sometimes singly, sometimes in pairs. Now they assumed a martyred air and stood on the outside and looked and looked. It was still very uncomfortable for the Moffats and the words, "Here come the Murdocks!" or, "I smell a Murdock!" were a signal for all of them to lock the doors quickly and hide behind curtains and chairs and not answer the doorbell and hope the Murdocks would go away.

Letitia was the most persistent of all the Murdocks. She would never go away. She would ring and ring and ring the doorbell. That evoking no response, she would run around to the back door and knock. You would think she'd wear her knuckles off the way she'd knock! That evoking no response, she would rap at whatever windows she could reach. Worse still, sometimes she would lean the stepladder against the house, shade her eyes with her palms, and peer intently within. Seeing no one about, she would hop down and wail, "Ja-ane!"

This would make Jane, who would be hiding under the yellow couch in the Grape Room, simply furious.

"Oh, why doesn't she go away?" she would say angrily to her doll, Hildegarde.

But the calls for Ja-ane would continue with the persistence of a fly buzzing around early in the morning. Then would follow a long welcome silence.

"There, she must have gone at last," the Moffats would say happily and begin to sally forth from their hide-outs, when the whole performance—knocking, rapping, peering, wailing, silence, would be begun all over again by the tireless Letitia.

Finally, after what seemed like hours of lurking in dark places, the Moffats would come forth defiantly, only to find the cause of their mole-like activities sitting on their hitching post sucking a lollipop. Letitia always had candy or something in a little paper bag. Of course she never dreamed of offering any of these good things to any of the Moffats.

Letitia's feelings never seemed in the least hurt by the Moffats' refusal to open the door to her. She entered into the whole thing as in a game which might be called "Trying-to-get-into-the-yellow-house." When on occasion she did manage to outwit her adversaries and actually gained entrance in the yellow house, she would scream triumphantly, "I got in!"

"Just don't pay any attention to her," the Moffats advised one another. "She'll get sick of hanging around and go home."

They would then go about their business and try to forget that Letitia was there.

One day Jane fetched her doll, Hildegarde, and her sewing and sat down on the thick grass by the lilac bush. It was time Hildegarde had a new dress. Janey sat with her back to the hitching post which always now seemed to have a Murdock on it. Janey was trying to ignore the fact that Letitia was sitting there right now, licking a lollipop. After a while she did forget about Letitia. She became lost in her own thoughts. It was a sweet-smelling day with the lilacs all blooming. Janey felt very happy.

A humming noise in the sky made her leap suddenly to her feet. An airplane!

Airplanes always excited Janey. Because she was always wishing she could fly.

She stood with her feet planted far apart to balance herself and she thrust her head back to get a good look at the plane. There it flew straight across the sky—a sky so blue it looked as though it had just been polished.

"Hi! Hi!" yelled Jane, waving her arms as the airplane passed above her and disappeared beyond the elm trees. Oh, wonderful! She wished she could fly, really fly! Not even in an airplane, but really. Well, she could fly down the stairs. At least she could go so fast down the stairs her feet did not touch at all from top to bottom Of course that was just in

her dreams.

But now, this minute, she wished she could fly or at least do something very extraordinary. Turn cartwheels, for instance. Why couldn't she at least turn cartwheels? Rufus could, over and over like a pinwheel. But she just couldn't. She always landed in the wrong position altogether. The hum of the plane's motor echoed in her ears. Flying! Imagine!

"Hildegarde," she said to her doll, "how would you like to fly like that? How would you like to go up in an airplane?"

Hildegarde simply stared with black unblinking eyes.

"Well," continued Jane, holding her high above her head, "now you are in an airplane. You are flying fast across the Nubian desert."

She let go of Hildegarde. She let go of the doll so she could go soaring across the sky. Did she soar across the sky? No! Instead, she crashed to the sidewalk. There she lay, head severed from body! For a moment Jane was stunned! Hildegarde! Then tears started to smart her eyes. But she swallowed her sobs. She didn't want to cry and have to explain how it was she had broken her doll.

"I thought you were in an airplane," she murmured as she gathered up the broken doll. "Why didn't you fly?" she added in exasperation.

She put the broken pieces in her sewing bag, thinking to herself, "Well, anyway, Hildegarde can be my Madame Bust for when I'm sewing for my dolls."

A whining voice from the hitching post startled her.

"Wha-ja-do? Break your doll?"

Jane regarded Letitia resentfully. It was horrible to think that anyone had been watching her, let alone that Letitia.

"Break your doll?" repeated Letitia.

"No!" shouted Jane, lying outrageously. And she resolved then and there to attempt to rid the yellow house of the dreadful Letitia for that day at least. A plan was already racing through her head. She ran around to the back yard to fetch Rufus whom she needed to help her carry it out. She quickly gave him his instructions. He proved a very willing and apt pupil. Presently he and Janey marched with solemn mien around the yard, past the front porch, and straight to Letitia.

"I am the great Houdini. I hypnotize people," Jane announced to Letitia. "I can hypnotize you, Rufus, or anybody else. I'm going to start on Rufus. I'll do it in a jiffy. Let me see—I think I'll make him think he is a dog."

With that, Jane wasted no time but adopted certain weird postures and passed her hands slowly before Rufus' face. She then began to chant in sepulchral tones,

"You are a dog. You are a dog. You are a dog."

Letitia watched with expressionless face.

"It takes a little while to get a person completely hyno-tized," Jane explained to Letitia.

"You are a dog. You are a dog," she repeated.

Rufus slowly wagged his rear end.

"See—it's beginning to work," said Jane to Letitia, "he's trying to wag his tail."

"You are a dog. You are a dog," she continued, making her gestures more mysterious and fearsome. "You are a dog. Now the spell is bound. Spell bound. Bark!" she screamed.

With this, Rufus fell to his knees, began to frisk about and bark. He enjoyed acting like a dog so much that his barks became more and more furious. He started nosing at Letitia's heels. He sounded like all the dogs of New Dollar Street, chasing and barking after a motorcycle. Indeed, several of these dogs, sensing excitement, ran out of their yards howling. Mrs. Squire ran to the window, rapped and scolded to no avail.

"Bow-wow," yelped Rufus, playfully seizing Letitia's sock in his teeth and pulling.

"Let go! Let go!" said Letitia. "Stop being a dog," she ordered him.

"Oh, he can't for you. Not till I un-hypnotize him."

"He'll tear my socks."

"That's too bad," said Jane politely.

"Woof-woof!" barked Rufus, grabbing at the hem of Letitia's skirt.

"He'll tear my dress," screamed Letitia.

"Just playful," murmured Jane delightedly.

"Go away," said Letitia, starting to kick at Rufus.

"Oh, don't hurt my little dog—or I shall hypnotize him into a lion," warned Jane.

"I got to go home," wailed Letitia.

"Oh, must you go so soon?" asked Jane mockingly. "What a great pity. Wouldn't you like me to hypnotize you too? Maybe if I changed you into a cat, my little dog could chase you up a tree."

And she started to strike hypnotic poses in front of

Letitia.

"You're a cat! You're a cat!" she started. But Letitia leaped down.

"Stop it! Stop it!" she yelled, running up the street with Rufus barking after her. Jane watched them and laughed to herself. Then she called Rufus back to the hitching post.

"Guess that got rid of her for once at least," said Jane triumphantly. "Hope she'll leave us alone for a while."

11

THE NEW SECOND AVENUE TROLLEY LINE

HURRAH! SCHOOL WAS ALL OVER UNTIL NEXT SEPTEMBER. Sylvie had left this morning for a week's vacation at Camp Lincoln. The other three children were on their way over to Sandy Beach, a small beach on the harbor at the other end of town altogether. They were going to spend the day there and had sandwiches and fruit for a picnic lunch. Mama was the only one left at home in the yellow house and she was sneezing her head off with hay fever and trying to finish a dress for Miss Chichester so the children might have another year at the dancing school.

The children loved to go to Sandy Beach. They loved to look out across the harbor that lay like a great pool of water at the feet of the Sleeping Giant and of East Rock and West Rock. They hoped to find a lot of the little pink and white shells. If they did they would make a necklace for Mama, Jane thought.

It used to be such a long walk over to Sandy Beach. So long that Rufus used to have to be dragged half the way in his express wagon, he'd get so tired. But now it was nothing to get there. The new Second Avenue trolley line whisked you there in just no time at all. If you were lucky, that is, and the motorman did not have to wait at the switch for the trolley that was coming from the other direction to get past him.

There was a switch at this end and a switch at the Sandy Beach end of the line. Sometimes the motorman was able to get all the way to the switch at the Sandy Beach end before the other trolley came along. That was when you were lucky. But more often than not the red light was on at this end of the line, the red light that said, "Hold! Wait there. Here comes the other car."

Then you had to wait so long you might just as well have walked in the first place. Still, the whole town agreed it was a fine thing, very modern, to have this new trolley line. Because the Sandy Beach end of town was so hard to reach otherwise. And you could bring a book or your knitting to pass the time when you had to wait at the switch.

"Here," Mama said as she kissed them good-by. "Here is a nickel for each one of you. Don't be gallivantin' all over town. Go straight to Sandy Beach and have a good time!" she called, waving her blue checked apron after them.

"Good-by," screamed Jane to Mama. "Don't let those Murdocks buy our house. Lock the doors and pretend you aren't home if they come back again."

"Come on, Jane," said Rufus, always impatient to be off. "What are you goin' to do with your five cents?"

Five cents apiece! They were of two minds as to what to do with it. They might spend it on an ice-cream cone or they might take the new Second Avenue trolley to Sandy Beach. Joe was all in favor of an ice-cream cone. Jane too. But Rufus had never been on the new Second Avenue trolley line. He preferred spending his five cents that way.

"I may be a motorman when I grow up," he said. "And

I'd like to see how they run."

"You've been on trolleys before," said Joe. "They all run alike."

"No," said Rufus. "There's this business about the red lights. I want to see how they handle that. There's two tracks everywhere else, 'n' there's just one track here. S'different."

"But I want a cone," said Joe.

"Well," said Rufus with finality. "I'm goin' to spend my five cents on the new Second Avenue line. I don't mind goin' alone."

"Oh, well. Let's all go that way then," said Jane. "It *is* fun to ride on the trolley and we'll have more time at the beach."

"All right," agreed Joe, although he still felt somewhat reluctant. However, later on, he was glad he had agreed to this because of the strange doings that followed.

The three sat down on the curb at Second Avenue to wait for the trolley. They picked the tinfoil out of several empty cigarette cases and chewing gum wrappers they found in the gutter. Joe rolled it up in a hard ball and put it in his pocket. Jane found a piece of colored red glass and they all took turns looking at one another and at the sky through this. When the trolley came, they got on and gave the motorman their five cent pieces. The motorman handed Rufus' five cents back to him.

"You don't have to pay, young man. Not till you're six," he said.

Well, six was just exactly what Rufus was now, but he saw no good in arguing the point at this moment. He put the five cents back in his pocket and gave Joe and Jane a rather triumphant glance.

There were very few people on the trolley. They were all sitting near the back and they were all very calm. Apparently they were quite accustomed to the new Second Avenue line and thought no more of riding on it than of the milkman delivering a bottle of milk every morning at their door. But Joe, Jane, and Rufus all sat in the front seat as near the motorman as possible. They looked at the signal at the side of the road. The light was green. Good! They would not have to wait for the trolley coming in the oppo-

site direction. The motorman started the car. But look! Just
as he stepped on the motor power, the red light flashed on!
It meant Stop! But did he stop? He did not! A baleful look
came over his face and he steered the car right off the switch
and onto the main track. What was the matter with the
man? The light said "Stop" and he went!

A murmur of surprise ran through the trolley. But the
motorman heeded this not at all. Up Second Avenue he
steered the trolley. stepping on the bell like anything every
time he saw a dog, and muttering to himself the whole way.
The children watched him in fascination.

"Makes me wait every time, does he?" he was saying to
himself. "Makes me wait every day down here. *He's* supposed to wait up there at the other switch once't in a while.
'I'll tell the chief,' I said to him. 'Tell the chief,' he said
to me. Tell the chief I did. 'Fight it out for yourself,' he
said to me. I'll show 'im! I'll show 'im!"

The children looked at one another. Excitement! They
looked ahead. Way, way down the car line, under the arch
of elm trees, they could see it now! Could see the other trolley coming right towards them! Just a little speck it was
at the other end of Second Avenue. But bigger and bigger

as it drew near. The nearer it came, the more excitedly the motorman clumped down on his bell. Pretty soon they were near enough to hear the other motorman clump down on *his* bell.

Although their hearts began to beat fast, Joe, Jane, and Rufus said and did nothing. The others in the trolley, roused out of their lethargy, first ran to the motorman and implored him to stop. But the motorman was deaf to all entreaties. So the passengers all ran to the back of the car to get as far as possible from what looked like an inevitable crash. Some uttered silent prayers.

And imagine what this looked like to people along Second Avenue! Windows were thrown up and amazed heads stuck out of them. Everybody on the street stopped to stare and wave their arms about in excitement. Old Mrs. Squire, who was carrying a basket of apples to her nephew, grew so frantic she actually threw apples at the motorman and screamed, "Go back, go back."

Such a thing was unheard of! Two trolleys on the same track, one going north, the other going south, could do only one thing—meet with a crash. And how ridiculous in broad daylight! If there were a fog now, like in London,

Louis Slobodkin

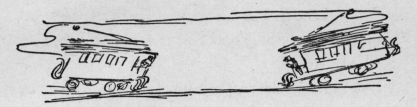

that would be a different matter; but broad daylight! That's
what all the people thought, anyway.

"Go back! Go back!" The cry was taken up by everyone
along the street, some running to one car, some to the other,
trying by emphatic waves of the arms to indicate what they
meant, as though the motormen were altogether deaf or
else quite daft. There was some talk of calling out the Fire
Department. Finally Mrs. Squire did sound the alarm. "A
hose will do much," she screamed.

All these people did not reckon, though, on the motorman. For he had a head on his shoulders. And so, for that
matter, did the enemy motorman. But how good his head
was and whether he'd choose to use it, that was the question.

The nearer the two cars came to one another the slower
they ran, although both motormen kept up that hullabaloo
of clumping down on the bells. Finally they were just edg-

ing towards one another like great tawny tigers at bay. At last they came to a dead stop, nose to nose, just as the hook and ladder arrived.

Now what would happen? Joe, Jane, and Rufus were shivery with tense excitement. Yes, it had required a great deal of nerve and trust in their motorman not to jump off when things looked so bad a while back.

"They oughta have pistols or a sword to fight it out," said Rufus.

But they didn't need pistols. Their tongues did quite well. Such a row there was as quiet Second Avenue had never before heard. Mrs. Squire said she would write a letter of complaint to the newspaper and recommend that the new Second Avenue line be removed. The town of Cranbury had gotten along for centuries without it and could again. Newfangled notions, these one-man trolleys with their one-track contraptions! But no one paid any attention to her. They were listening to the motormen. Except for the firemen of course. They were crawling over and under the two trolleys looking for the fire. And everyone was listening too hard to what the motormen were saying to tell them that there was no fire.

The Moffats' motorman was an old man with a walrus mustache. He wore his hat straight over his eyes and took this business of driving a trolley car very seriously. The enemy trolley had a young motorman who wore his hat tipped on the back of his head and sat all slouchy on his stool. Yes, the picture of impudence.

"Hey, you old sardine, you!" he bawled in a most insulting tone of voice. "You were supposed to wait. What's a matter with your eyes? Didn't ya see the red light?"

"Yeh, you young whippersnapper. I saw the light all right, all right. Same's I do every trip. And I'm sick of seein' those red lights, see? You're supposed to wait up there at the upper switch half the time. At least until two-thirty. Do you ever do it? No, you do not. My people wants to git home, just as much as your'n wants to be off. It's a fifty-fifty proposition. Now back up your car to the other switch or I'll . . ."

And he edged his car an inch nearer, menacingly.

"Why, you old sardine . . ." sputtered the other.

More angry words followed but the young motorman could see the old one would never yield an inch. On the contrary, he was getting in such a dither he was all but climbing out of the front end of his trolley to shake his fist in the other man's face. Goodness knows what a man of his temperament might not do. Moreover, the worst of it was the old geezer was right. Chief had just said to him the other day, "Look here, O'Brien. On the two-thirty trolley you're supposed to wait for old McCann at the upper switch until two-thirty on the dot. If he's not there then, you can go. Otherwise wait, get me?"

Oh, it was clear the young motorman did not have a leg to stand on. Moreover, the sentiment of all the onlookers was on the old motorman's side. So he said, "All right, you old sardine, you. But you'll hear from the Chief about this. Endangerin' the lives of the citizens of Cranbury, that's what it amounts to."

Then he tipped his hat still farther back on his forehead. He assumed an air of great nonchalance and took the driving gear to the other end of his trolley. The firemen cleared the way, and Motorman O'Brien, defeated, started back the way he had come, old McCann following close behind, all but butting him in the rear like an angry bull. The people cheered. The firemen sounded their siren and went back to the firehouse. Mrs. Squire looked around for some of her apples to take to her nephew, but the little boys had gotten most of them. The yellow dogs ran up the street after the yellow trolleys, yelping and growling.

At last the enemy O'Brien's trolley was safely lodged on the side switch and the Moffats' trolley sailed triumphantly up the track to Sandy Beach where Joe, Jane, and Rufus got off. Phew! That had been a ride and worth a nickel, if not more!

THE NEW SECOND AVENUE TROLLEY LINE

Nothing that happened that afternoon—swimming, ducking, digging for clams, catching snails—nothing could come up to that trolley ride. That trolley ride! There was something to tell Mama about!

12

THE LAST CHAPTER IN THE YELLOW HOUSE

THE MOFFATS WERE MOVING! THEY WERE GOING TO LIVE in a different house on a different street altogether. Yes, it was really so! The yellow house had been sold! Those Murdocks did buy it! So this was the last, the very last day in the yellow house. No wonder everybody was going around with a lump in his throat. But there was also a feeling of expectancy and excitement. This was the way it happened finally that the sign had come down and that they had to move.

Joe, Jane, and Rufus were on their way home from an afternoon at Sandy Beach. They had spent so many hours there this summer that Rufus' naturally dark skin was darker than ever, though Joe and Jane were pink and peeling. As they turned from Elm Street into New Dollar Street their steps quickened. As always, it felt good to be going home to the yellow house, to kiss Mama, to smell what was cooking for supper. Oh, they could hardly wait— and although they were tired from the long walk home, they had broken into a run when they passed Chief Mulligan's house.

"Beat you home," shouted Jane, and they all raced up the street, past the Pudges', past the Frosts', past the Shoemakers', past the disapproving Mrs. Squire's, and with a whoop through the gate of their own yellow house. There they stopped short. The sign was down! The For Sale sign which they hated so, but which they knew, while it was still tacked up there, meant they could live in the yellow house, the sign was down!

"It's gone!" screamed Jane.

"The sign's down!" said Joe.

"Mama," yelled Rufus.

Mama met them at the door. She drew them all to her in a huge hug.

"Yes," she said. "The sign is down! The house has sold! And who do you think bought it? Of course. Those Murdocks! Dr. Witty was here this afternoon and he tore down the sign. 'Well,' he said, 'the house has sold! Thank goodness!' he said. And he said he was very sorry to lose us as tenants. He was very nice but still he said we would have to move. He gave us one month to look for another place. Now don't feel too badly. You know we have sort of known this was bound to happen all year long."

It was true. They had sort of known it. And yet they couldn't help feeling stunned. Rufus didn't remember living in any other house. He had learned to talk, learned to walk, and had five birthdays and five Christmases in this house. Jane had made paper dolls, studied through the thirteen colonies in school, knew every inch of this house except the little-used dirt cellar, and had flown down the stairs hundreds of times even if it was just in her dreams. And Joe and Sylvie, although they remembered the old house across the way and remembered Papa too, they had always felt this yellow house would be theirs forever. But wasn't a month a long way off?

"How long is a month?" asked Rufus. "As far as Christmas?"

And everyone was glad of an excuse to laugh. Otherwise they might have cried. Certainly Janey might have.

But now today the month had gone! It was the last day. Mama had found another house. It was a tiny little house set far back from the street so that it had a long front lawn and almost no back yard. Mama did not like this business about the yards. "There we sit in everybody's back yard," she said. And at first the children had not liked it either. "Imagine," they said. "Hardly any apple trees at all and only one grape arbor." And Joe mopped his forehead when he thought of mowing all that long green lawn in front. But Jane was rather charmed with the long green carpet at the end of which was their tiny little house. It was some-how like looking through the wrong end of a telescope

In their hearts all the Moffats knew there might be many things about the new little house that they would like, but today, right now, while these things were still unknown to them, they all had huge lumps in their throats.

They had all spent the day in packing up. At last all was practically ready. Madame was on the porch wearing a rather disapproving air. The broom was leaning against her. The furniture was grouped in corners of the rooms and the carpets were rolled up. The pipes had been taken down from the kitchen stove and the little stove in the sitting-room. They were all waiting for the moving van.

From time to time the children walked through the empty rooms, feeling strange. The yellow house was no longer their home. Later on it would live in their memories alive and glowing again like the coals that used to fall in the grates. But now, today, it was unfamiliar. Their footsteps echoed on the wooden floors. Where the pictures had hung were clean squares of wall-paper. Every so often one or another of the four Moffats ran to steal a look at Mama to see if she too had changed.

Joe wandered off to the back yard. He wanted to climb that old apple tree once more. Rufus shinned up the cherry

 tree, the one he had fallen out of the year before last. Sylvie made some last-minute entries in her diary. Perhaps she was writing about how it felt to be moving away from this house she had lived in so long, thought Jane. Or maybe she was writing about that week's vacation she'd had at Camp Lincoln. Jane wished she knew. But there—Sylvie kept her diary locked.

Mama was still packing the last few things in the pantry; the china Jersey cow that could be used either for a bank or a milk pitcher; the porcelain head of a man—lift his hat off and keep tobacco in it. That's what it was meant for, anyway, although Mama used it for spices. "And the funny thing about it," said Mama to Jane who was feeling closer and closer to tears, "the funny thing about it is that it looks very much like your father looked when he was courting me. Mustache and all."

When Mama finished with these last few things, she said, "I wonder what is keeping the moving man. Jane, would you mind running over to I. Bimber's, the moving van company, and tell them we are ready?"

No. Jane was glad to have something definite to do.

She started running up the street. She passed Mrs. Pudge who was walking slowly up the street to the trolley car. Mrs. Pudge called after her, "So you're moving today, Jane?"

Jane nodded, bobbing her braids up and down importantly. She found a stone and kicked it with the blunt toe of her brown sandal. She kept kicking it ahead of her, playing a game she made up; if it landed on the right side of the pavement more often than the left, it would turn into a nugget of gold.

At the same time she was thinking that some day she too would be too old to run up the street and race with the trolley cars. She would have to walk like Mrs. Pudge. How could she bear that? And how could she bear never to play cops and robbers with the boys? Or never to walk fences? Or never to play baseball in the vacant lot? Imagine Mrs. Pudge or Mrs. Ellenbach or any of the other women on New Dollar Street doing these things. But Jane had a feeling that just as surely as that they, the Moffats, were moving away from the yellow house that day, time would take these other keen delights from her too.

Why, you just had to look at Sylvie to see that this was true. Sylvie still liked to race up the street. But she never played cops and robbers any more, and some day she would probably get married. Then who would take care of her

chilblains and sing her to sleep, Janey wondered, giving the stone a terrific kick which lodged it between a tree and a fence.

She stopped and worked at it with her toe. Finally it bounded out and she kicked it hard right straight in front of her.

"Besides," she thought, "nothing ever divides into threes well 's fours."

And would Catherine-the-cat know enough to bring only three kittens instead of the usual four when Sylvie married and left them to set up housekeeping like Tilly Cadwalader?

Well, these thoughts did not take the lump out of her throat. On the contrary, she had the utmost difficulty restraining those foolish tears when she told Mr. Bimber they were waiting for the van.

"Baby!" she whispered furiously to herself when she left.

Instead of going right back to the yellow house, Jane decided to walk over to the new house a few blocks away to see again how it looked.

When she got there, she bent over and looked at the little house from between her legs. It looked quite charming and rather like a picture post-card. Straightening up she walked around the little back yard.

"Hardly a tree in it," she observed gloomily.

She stepped onto the little porch that was covered with hop vines. She looked through the window. The rooms were empty but they wore a look of expectancy. There were a dustpan and brush in one corner. Mama had been here yesterday cleaning up. Would this place ever seem like home, Jane wondered.

She went down the long path to the street. "I'll pretend I'm comin' home from school," she said, "and see how it feels."

She skipped up the path singing at the top of her lungs "I saw you toss the kites on high," the way she always did when she came home from school to the yellow house. She ran around to the back door, pushed it open, and sniffed.

It was no use. This house had a musty smell and seemed neither friendly nor unfriendly, just indifferent.

"After all," she reflected, "it's still empty. When we all get in it, it'll be different maybe."

Slowly she went out of the house into the back yard. She climbed the fence that separated this yard from the neighbor's and sat there. The branches of an apple tree in the yard behind theirs sheltered her. Two tears trickled down her cheeks. Life would be different in this house. Suddenly a voice startlingly near her said:

"Are you crying? I never cry unless it's something just frightfully important."

"I'm not crying," denied Jane indignantly. She looked around to see who it was that had caught her.

There was no one in sight, no one down in either of the yards below. A mocking laugh made her look up. She caught her breath. A girl about her own age was sitting on a high branch of the tree. It was her hair that made Jane catch her breath. A head of tangled curls of gold just like the ones she herself had in her dreams.

She almost fell off the fence in her surprise.

"Ha-ha," laughed the girl heartily. "Surprised you, didn't I? Say, are you by any chance going to move into this house?"

"Yes," said Jane, very shy.

"Oh! Well, that's good. How old are you?"

"Ten."

"So am I. I live in that house back there. This is my back yard. What's your name?"

"Jane Moffat."

"Mine's Nancy Stokes. Well, I'm glad you're moving in here. My best friend, Alice Phelps, moved away last week. We used to have plenty of good fights. Perhaps if I like you and you like me, we can get to be best friends."

Best friends! Jane had never had a best friend before. There had always been just the four of them—Sylvie, Joe, Jane, and Rufus. Oh, of course, she had friends too. There were Chief Mulligan, Mr. Brooney, her teacher, and she often went hunting wild flowers with Milly Cadwalader, but she had never had a best friend. What was it like to have a best friend? She didn't know what to say.

"How many in your family?" Nancy went on. "There's just myself and Bee, my sister. And of course Mother and

Dad."

"In mine there's Sylvie, Joe, me, and Rufus. And Mama and Catherine-the-cat."

"Well, I think it's great you're moving here. We'll build a gate in this fence if Mother'll let us."

"Yes," agreed Jane, still shy.

"Say! What do you think about before you go to sleep?"

Jane was silent. A princess with golden curls. A prince on a black horse riding down a wooded path. A meeting in the clearing by the cold, clear spring. These were the things she thought about before she went to sleep.

"I mean, what do you dream you are before you go to sleep?" Nancy was insistent. Jane felt she had to answer.

"I think I'm a princess with long golden curls ridin' on a white horse."

"You do!" The girl seemed surprised.

Jane felt overwhelmed with shyness. Goodness, that wasn't the thing to think about at all, she thought. Had she blasted her chance of being best friends? She felt like flying away.

"Well," Nancy went on, "I dream I'm a great singer. I'm on the platform and all the theater is clapping and clapping."

Her eyes shone. Jane was thrilled. She saw this girl on
the stage of the Metropolitan Opera House like the other
great singers Mama had told her about. And she, Jane, was
going to be her best friend! An incredible feeling of happiness gushed up in her. She wished she could think of something to say. Instead, she picked a leaf from the tree and
started to chew on it.

Suddenly the girl swung herself out of the tree. "Well,
so long," she said. "I've got to have my music lesson. See
you later." And she walked off, whistling.

Jane followed her with her eyes as long as she could see
her. The girl went into the big house whose yard backed
up to her yard. Jane was still tingling inside. Best friends!
She jumped off the fence and tore back to the yellow house
like lightning.

I. Bimber's moving van was already there. Jane sat on
the hitching post and watched. Joe and Rufus sat on Mrs.
Squire's wire fence. Mrs. Squire was sitting behind the parlor curtains, watching proceedings herself. Today she did
not seem to mind that Rufus and Joe were sitting on her
fence. "Those Moffats are moving away and it will be nice

and quiet here. If only Peter Frost and the Pudges would move away too, and all those Cadwaladers, New Dollar Street wouldn't be so bad."

Sylvie was racing around helping Mama. Sylvie's curls were caught up in the back. "Just like a grown-up," thought Jane.

I. Bimber's men came out with load after load. First they piled everything on the sidewalk so that people had to walk out in the street to get by, even Chief Mulligan of the police force. Then they stored things neatly in the van, covering each piece with an old quilt. The last to go in were Madame and the little pot-bellied stove. These were bound fast to the wagon with thick ropes.

Madame was placed with her back to the pot-bellied stove. She seemed disdainful. Such company to be keeping! She is fat where he is thin, thought Jane, laughing out loud. And he is fat where she is thin. They are going on their honeymoon, she thought, and already they have had a slight disagreement.

But now everything was ready. The moving men mopped their brows. One took a fresh chew of tobacco.

"Get on," they said. For all the Moffats were going to

ride to the new house with them.

Jane jumped down from the hitching post. She joined
Mama who was banging the green shutters with a firm
hand. The back door was already locked and now Mama
locked the front door.

"Have I forgotten anything?" she asked.

They stopped for a moment and thought. No. Nothing
had been forgotten. Nothing left behind. They went out
to the van. Joe and Rufus were already sitting on the back,
right under the little stove and Madame. Janey climbed
up beside them and Mama climbed up beside the driver.
Sylvie ran around from the back yard. In her hand were
sprigs of green things she would transplant in the new
yard. She climbed up and sat on the ironing board. Now
they were ready to go.

The driver said "Giddap" to the team.

Suddenly Mama said, "Who-a! Where is Catherine-the-
cat?"

There she was, that cat, sitting in the pear tree, looking
at them all with intense disapproval. Joe jumped off to
catch her. She did not like all this upset and confusion.
She arched her back at Joe and she absolutely refused to

come. Mama leaned out of the wagon.

"Catherine, come here," she commanded. And Catherine obeyed. Mama was one person she always obeyed. She did not come in a straight path, but she came. She skulked along the house and then along the fence, and finally landed at the moving van, her head looking suspiciously to left and right. She leaped into the cold grate of the kitchen stove and there she sat, glowering.

Now they really were off! The team backed up. Then it started creaking and groaning up the street. The children waved at the yellow house.

"Good-by, good-by," they sang. Again there were lumps in their throats, but they didn't cry. They were sad but they were excited too. They were moving! Moving to something different.

They waved their handkerchiefs until they turned the corner from New Dollar Street into Elm Street. Now they could no longer see the yellow house. Good-by, yellow house! Good-by!

THE
END